漫画中国思想系列
Chinese Thought Comic Series

自然的箫声

庄子说

ZHUANG ZI SPEAKS
The Music of Nature

蔡志忠 ／编绘

[美] 布莱恩·布雅 ／译

中国出版集团
现代出版社

图字：01-2005-0835

图书在版编目（CIP）数据

庄子说 / 蔡志忠编绘；（美）布雅（Bruya, B.）译.
-- 北京：现代出版社, 2013.8
（蔡志忠漫画中国传统文化经典：中英文对照版）
ISBN 978-7-5143-1661-2

Ⅰ．①庄… Ⅱ．①蔡… ②布… Ⅲ．①漫画-连环画-作品集-中国-现代 Ⅳ．① J228.2

中国版本图书馆CIP数据核字（2013）第 181219 号

蔡志忠漫画中国传统文化经典：中英文对照版

庄子说

作　　者	蔡志忠　编绘
	［美］布莱恩·布雅（BRIAN BRUYA）译
责任编辑	袁　涛
出版发行	现代出版社
地　　址	北京市安定门外安华里 504 号
邮政编码	100011
电　　话	010-64267325　010-64245264（兼传真）
网　　址	www.1980xd.com
电子信箱	xiandai@cnpitc.com.cn
印　　刷	三河市南阳印刷有限公司
开　　本	710×1000　1/16
印　　张	16.25
版　　次	2013年9月第1版　2017年1月第7次印刷
书　　号	ISBN 978-7-5143-1661-2
定　　价	28.00元

版权所有，翻印必究；未经许可，不得转载

目录 contents

庄子说·自然的箫声（上篇）
Zhuangzi Speaks I   The Music of Nature 1
庄子
Zhuangzi 2
寒蝉和灵龟　The Winter Cicada and the Wonder Tortoise 6
小麻雀的得意　The Little Sparrow's Small Happiness 8
惠施的大葫芦　Hui Shi's Giant Gourd 9
宋人的秘方　The Song Family's Secret Formula 11
无用的樗树　The Useless Shu Tree 13
越人文身　The Tattooed Yue People 16
大地的箫声　The Music of the Earth 17
昭文不再弹琴　Zhao Wen Quits the Zither 20
王倪知道不知道　Does Wang Ni Know? 21
西施是美女吗　Is Xi Shi Really Beautiful? 23
丽姬的哭泣　Li Ji's Tears 24
长梧子的大梦　Zhang Wuzi's Dream 25
影子的对话　Dialogue With a Shadow 26
庄周梦见蝴蝶　The Dream of the Butterfly 27
朝三暮四　Three at Dawn and Four at Dusk 28
惠施靠在梧桐上　Hui Shi Leans Against a Tree 29
庖丁解牛　Paoding Carves Up a Cow 30
薪尽火传　Passing on the Flame 32
笼中的野鸡　The Caged Chicken 33
螳臂当车　The Mantis Stops a Cart 34
爱马的人　The Horse Lover 36
土地神的树　The Earth Spirit's Tree 37
树的天年　A Tree's Natural Life Span 39

不可想象的怪人	The Freak	41
油把自己烧干了	Oil Burns Itself Out	42
养虎的人	The Tiger Trainer	43
没有脚指头的废人	Toeless Shu	44
自然是超级英雄	Nature the Superhero	45
人相忘于道术	Forgetting the Dao	46
子桑唱贫穷之歌	Zi Sang Questions His Fate	47
海中凿河	Digging a Hole in the Ocean Floor	48
鸭脚太短吗	Are a Duck's Legs Too Short?	49
牧羊人丢了羊	The Lost Goat	50
盗亦有道	Thieves Have Principles, Too	51
赵国的美酒	Good Wine, Bad Wine	53
黄帝问道广成子	The Emperor Goes to Guang Chengzi	54
自然的友	Nature's Friend	55
做车轮的老人	The Old Wheelwright	56
天地日月	The Earth and the Sky	58
海鸥和乌鸦	Crows and Seagulls	59
孔子看到龙	Confucius Sees a Dragon	60
不要穿牛鼻	Don't Ring the Bull's Nose	61
风和蛇	The Wind and the Snake	62
圣人的勇气	Courage of the Sage	64
井底之蛙	The Frog in the Well	66
邯郸学步	Learning How to Walk in Handan	69
鸦乌吃腐鼠	A Crow Eating a Dead Rat	70
子非鱼安知鱼之乐	You're Not a Fish	72
庄子梦见骷髅	Zhuangzi Dreams of a Skeleton	73
海鸟不爱音乐	Sea Birds Don't Like Music	75
酒醉驾车的人	The Drunk Passenger	77
浮游于道德	Riding with Nature	78
甘泉先竭	The Sweet Water is Gone First	80
林回弃璧	Lin Hui Forsakes a Fortune	82
燕子结巢梁上	Swallows Nest in the Eaves	83
螳螂捕蝉	The Mantis Getting the Cicada	84

凡国不曾灭亡	Fan Was Never Destroyed	86
知识和大道	Knowledge and the Dao	87
庚桑楚逃名	Geng Sangchu Forsakes Fame	89
黄帝问道于牧童	The Yellow Emperor and the Pastureboy	90
石匠和郢人	The Stone Mason and the Ying Man	92
蜗牛角上的两国	Two Nations on a Snail's Antennae	94
庄周贷粟	Zhuangzi Borrows Grain	95
灵验的白龟	The Turtle That Could Predict the Future	96
自然的用	Natural Use	98
得鱼忘荃	After Catching the Fish, Discard the Trap	99
杨朱学道	Yang Zhu Studies the Dao	100
子贡衣服雪白	Zi Gong's Snow White Clothes	101
大盗的大道理	The Villain Speaks	103
庄子三剑	Zhuangzi's Three Swords	108
孔子游黑森林	Confucius in the Black Forest	115
讨厌脚迹的人	The Man Who Hated His Footprints	118
讨厌影子的人	The Man Who Hated His Shadow	119
泛若不系之舟	Like a Drifting Boat	120
屠龙之技	The Dragonslayer	121
打碎龙珠	Shattering the Dragonpearl	123
不做牺牲	Don't Make Sacrifices	125
庄子快死了	Zhuangzi on His Deathbed	126

庄子说·自然的箫声（下篇）
Zhuangzi Speaks II More Music of Nature ... 127

庄子	Zhuangzi	128
巨大的怪鸟	The Giant Bird	129
列子御风而行	Liezi Rides the Wind	130
许由不受天下	Xu You Refuses the World	131
谁是主宰	Who's the Master?	132
庄子说话不说话	Zhuangzi Speaks about Not Speaking	133
尧问	Yao's Question	134
养生主	The Danger of Knowledge	135

一只脚的人	The Man With One Leg	136
秦失不哭泣	Qin Shi Didn't Cry	137
颜回心斋	Mental Fasting	138
饮冰的人	The Man on Fire	139
楚狂人接舆	The Madman of Chu	140
形体与精神	Body and Spirit	141
人是无情的吗	Do People Have Emotions?	142
何谓真人	What is a Genuine Person	143
道比天高	The Dao is Higher Than Heaven	144
相忘于江湖	Mindless of Each Other	145
藏天下于天下	Hiding the World in the World	146
自然的生灭	Creation and Destruction	147
颜回坐忘	Yan Hui Sits in Forgetting	149
至人用心若镜	The Mind is Like a Mirror	151
浑沌之死	The Death of Primal Chaos	152
第六只手指	The Sixth Finger	153
大惑易性	Great Confusion Alters One's Nature	154
伯乐的罪过	The Horse Trainer's Transgressions	155
仁义之害	The Harm of Benevolence and Righteousness	157
防盗术	Theft Prevention	158
黄帝遗失玄珠	The Lost Pearl	159
天道	The Heavenly Dao	161
无为而治	Governing Through Non-Action	162
无江海而闲	Independent Leisure	163
养神贵精	Energy and Spirit	165
不住山林的隐士	Recluses	166
秋水	Autumn Waters	167
天地与毫毛	Heaven and Earth and a Strand of Fur	169
大小和极限	Size and Limits	170
大道和贵贱	Status and the Dao	171
谢施	Alternating Functions	172
不怕水火	Fire Doesn't Burn	173
污泥中的龟	A Turtle in the Muck	174

至乐	Ultimate Joy	175
庄子鼓盆	Zhuangzi Drums on a Pot	177
柳生左肘	A Lump on the Elbow	179
人不生不灭	People Neither Live Nor Die	180
至人之境	Realm of the Perfect Person	181
黏蝉的老人	Catching Cicadas	182
操舟如神	Steering a Boat	184
祭盘上的牺牲	The Sacrificial Pigs	186
瀑布下游泳的人	Swimming in a Waterfall	187
梓庆做钟架	Qing Makes a Bell-Stand	188
东野稷盘马	Dongye Ji Has an Accident	189
工倕的手指	Gong Chui's Fingers	190
庄子在荆棘中	Zhuangzi in the Brambles	191
鲁国只有一个儒者	Only One Confucian in Lu	192
百里奚养牛	Baili Xi Raises Oxen	194
真正的画师	The Genuine Painter	195
至人之箭	Perfect Archery	196
爵禄无变于己	Self-Respect	198
道可以拥有吗	Can the Dao Be Possessed?	199
道在屎溺	The Dao in Defecation	200
道超越知	The Dao Transcends Knowledge	202
心无旁骛	No Distractions	204
知的极点	Breaking the Barriers	205
至仁	Ultimate Benevolence	206
徐无鬼相狗相马	Xu Wugui's Appraisals	207
诗书六艺不如狗马经	The Exile	209
吴王射巧猿	The King Kills a Special Monkey	211
不知的境域	The Realm of Ignorance	212
环中之道	The Cyclic Dao	213
任公子钓大鱼	The Prince of Ren Goes Fishing	214
孔子的变化	Confucius Changes	215
无牵挂的人	No Attachments	216
得道的阶段	The Phases of Attaining the Dao	217
生活为贵名位为轻	Life Is Most Important	218

屠羊人不居功　The Goat Butcher Refuses Reward 219
颜回不做官　Refusing Office 220
逐利之夫　The Man Who Pursued Profit 221

附录·延伸阅读
APPENDIX Further reading 222

庄子说·自然的箫声
（上篇）

Zhuangzi Speaks I
The Music of Nature

庄子
Zhuangzi

庄子说　自然的箫声

庄子名周，战国时代宋国人。那是一个强凌弱，众暴寡、离乱、痛苦的时代，现实世界的痛苦，是一个无底的陷阱，丘垄黄土下的贤者，是伟大？还是渺小？
The name of our hero is Zhuang Zhou, and like all Chinese names, the surname comes first, followed by the given name. To show respect for his vast wisdom, we add the word zi to his surname, just like Kongzi (Confucius), Mengzi (Mencius), and Laozi. Zhuangzi lived during the fourth century B.C., a time known as the Warring States period in China. This was a period of disunity in which rival nations battled constantly for more land and greater power. As a result, it was also a time or widespread death and destruction. Zhuangzi saw this and was deeply saddened by it.

庄子的视线，从此自人世移开，他所综观的乃是无穷的时空。
As a way out, Zhuangzi shifted his line of sight from the earthly world to the limitlessness of time and space.

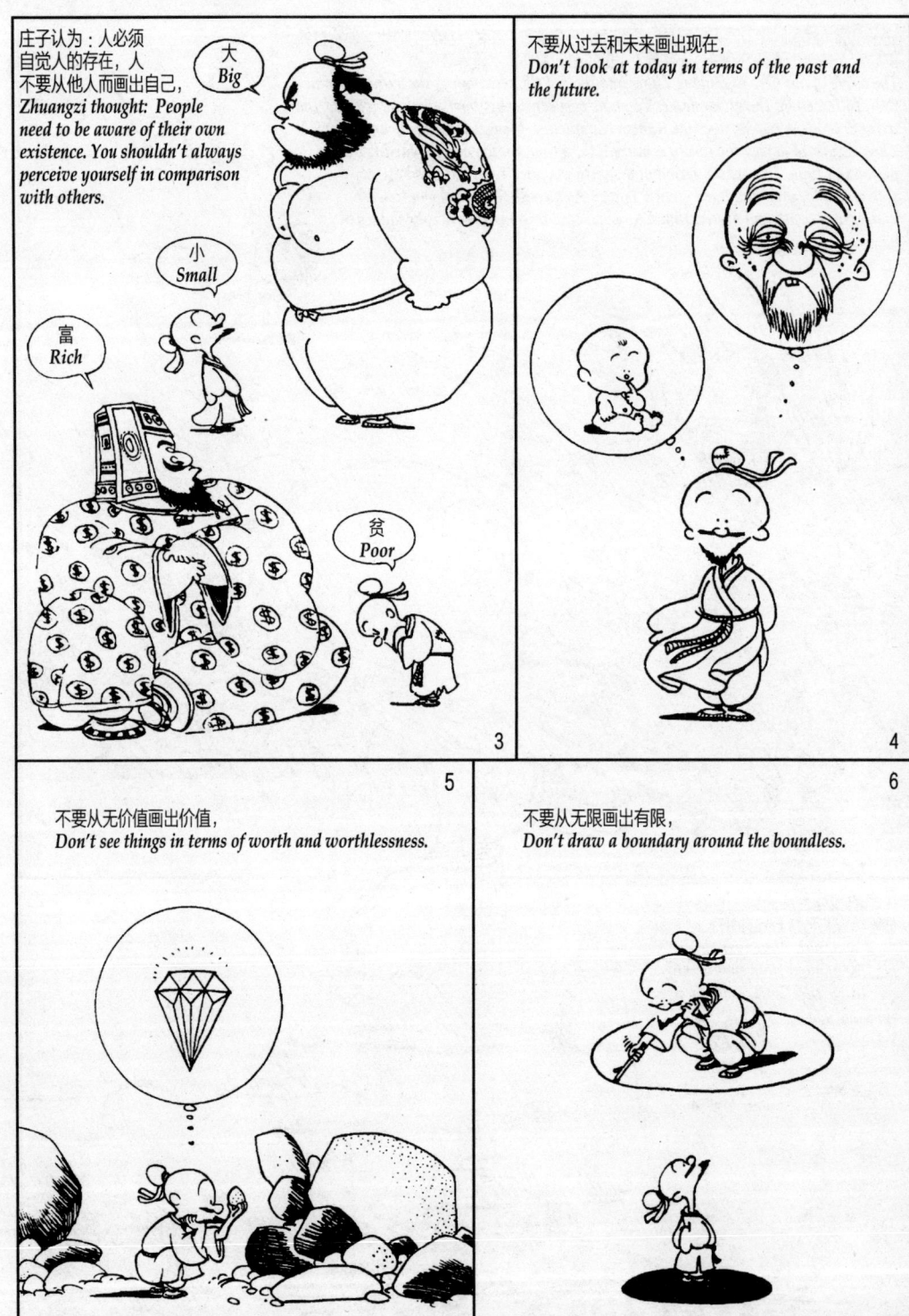

蔡志忠　漫画中国传统文化经典

寒蝉和灵龟
The Winter Cicada and the Wonder Tortoise

1. 世人都说彭祖活了八百岁，是人间最长寿的了。
People say that once there was a man named Peng Zu, who at 800 years old had lived the longest life ever.

哇噻好长寿！ You can say that again!

人瑞！ Wow, he is old!

2. 但有一种小虫叫做"朝菌"，朝生而暮死，
In contrast, there is a small bug called the Zhaojun that is born in the morning and is dead by nightfall.

3. 它根本不知道什么叫"一个月"。
It doesn't even know what a month is.

4. 另外有一种虫叫"寒蝉"，春生而夏死……
There is also an insect called the winter cicada, which is born in the Spring and dies in the Summer.

5. 它根本不知道什么叫"四季"。
It doesn't even know what the four seasons are.

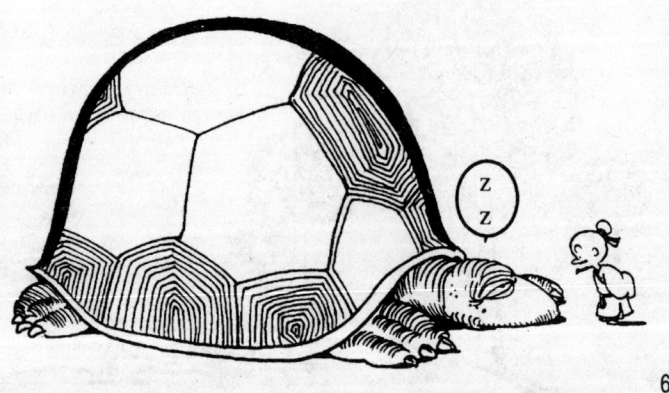

6. 可是楚国南方的海上有一只巨大的灵龟，五百年对它只是一个春季，五百年对它只是一个秋季。
However, in the southern part of Chu, there lived the giant wonder tortoise, to whom five hundred years was a mere Spring.

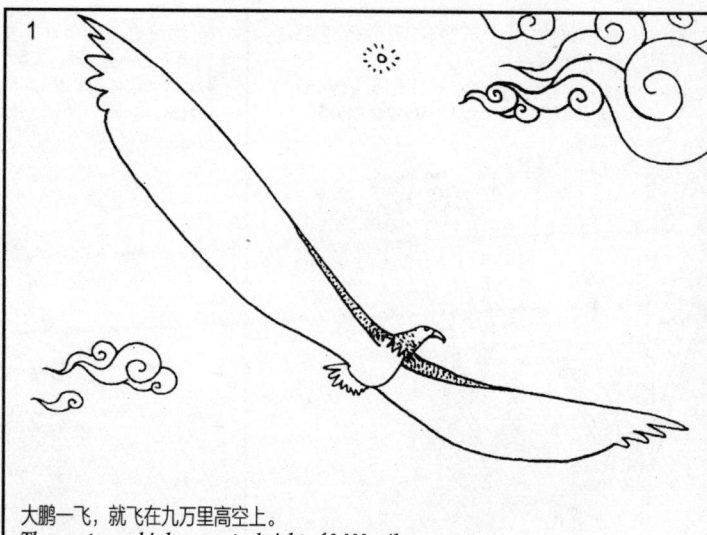
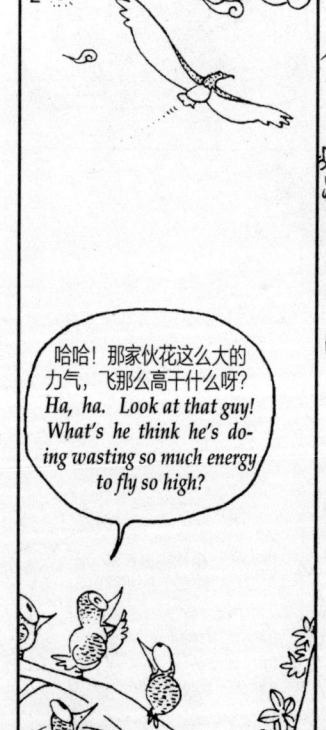

庄子说　自然的箫声

宋人的秘方
The Song Family's Secret Formula

宋国有一族人善于制造一种药，
In the State of Song, there lived a family who knew how to make a certain kind of medicine.

这种药，冬天的时候搽在皮肤上，可使皮肤不会干裂。
This medicine could protect the skin from cracking and chaffing during the dry winter.

所以这一族人，世世代代便做漂白布絮的生意。
Keeping this medicine to themselves, generation after generation of the Song family did a business in cloth bleaching.

后来有个客人知道了，便出百金，收购了这个秘方。
Then one day, a traveler found out about the formula for the medicine and bought it for one hundred gold pieces.

真是宝物！
This is worth a fortune!

他将秘方献给吴王，并说明这个秘方在军事上的秘用。
He presented the secret formula to the king of Wu and explained its use.

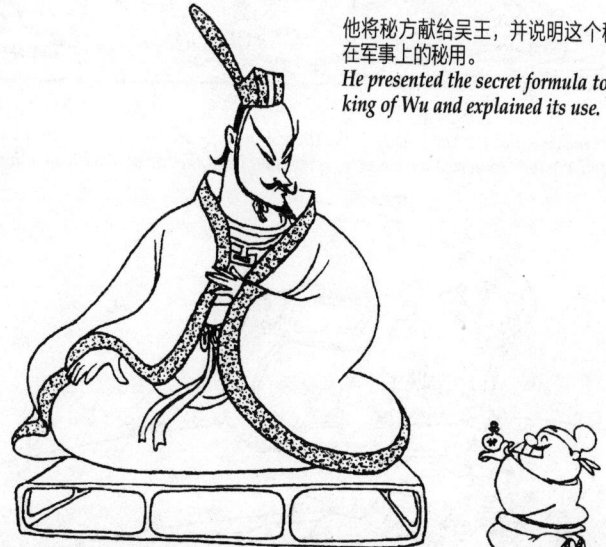

越人文身
The Tattooed Yue People

有一个宋国人，带着帽子和衣服到南方的越国去贩卖，他以为可以赚到一笔大钱……
One day, a man from Song went to Yue to sell hats and shirts, thinking he could make lots of money.

来买衣服吧！漂亮又新潮的衣帽呀！
Get yer shirts! Beeyooteeful hats and shirts for sale!

但是，越人的风俗是：剪断了头发，赤裸着身子，身上刺画着文彩，全不穿戴衣帽。
What he didn't know was that the Yue people had a custom of cutting their hair short and not wearing shirts because they tattooed their bodies.

没有用的衣帽。
Useless stuff.

用和无用，功和无功，都是相对的，不可执着不化。尧舜的"有功无功"和宋人的衣帽"有用无用"都同样不是绝对的。
Useful and useless, achievement and failure, are all relative, and none are necessarily consistent over time. The achievement and failure of the ancient kings Yao and Shun are like the usefulness and uselessness of the Song man's garments, nothing is for sure.

有用 Useful　　无用 Useless

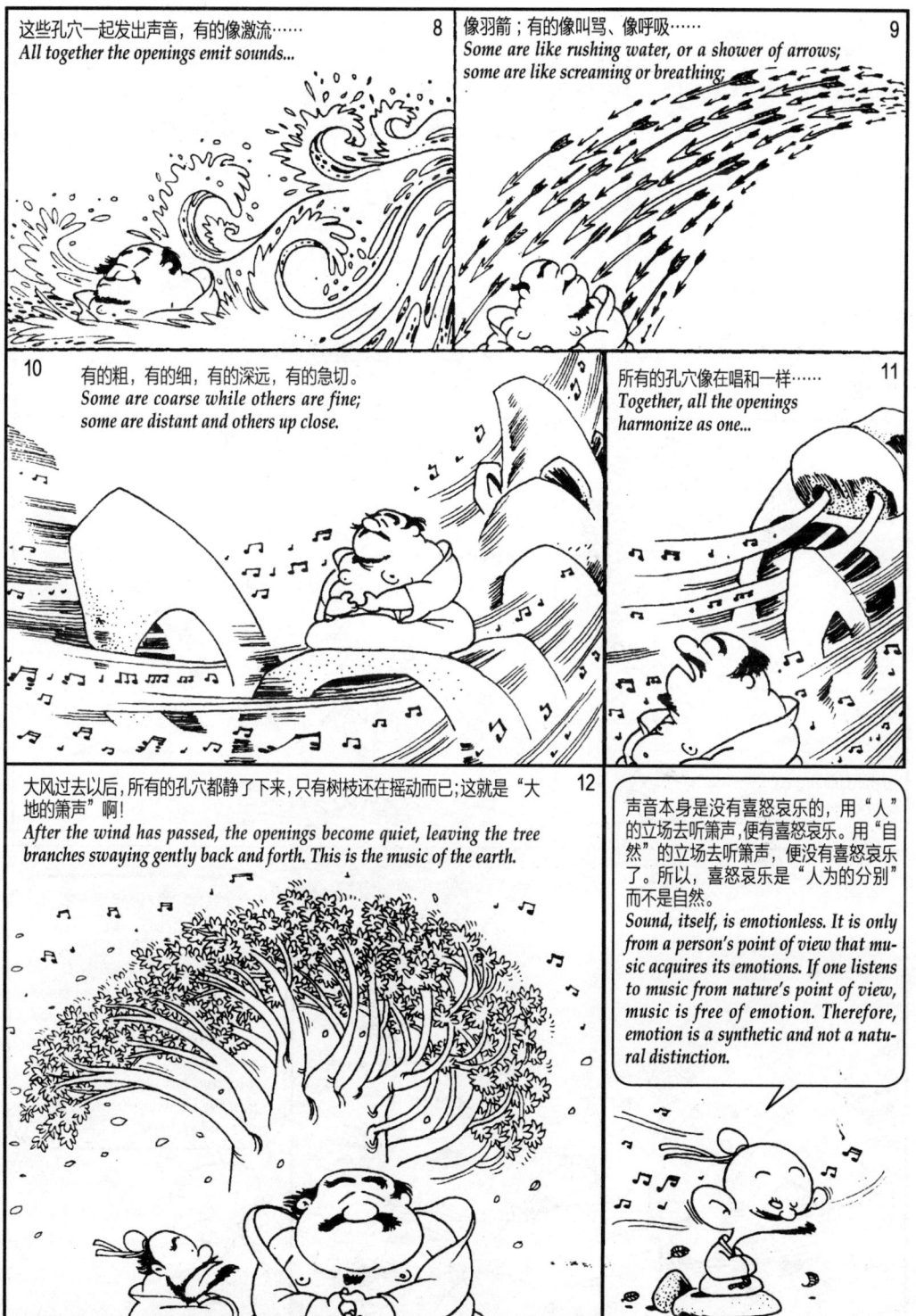

昭文不再弹琴
Zhao Wen Quits the Zither

昭文是有名的琴师,他的琴弹得非常好。
Once there was a famous Zither player named Zhao Wen, who could play the Zither like no one else.

但是,后来昭文再也不弹琴了。
But one day, Zhao Wen suddenly stopped playing the zither altogether.

因为他终于悟到:弹琴的时候,只要发出一个声音,便失掉了其他的声音……
He finally realized that in playing one sound, it would be to the neglect of all the other sounds...

只有在住手不弹的时候,才能五音俱全。
It was only when he wasn't playing, that he could hear everything in complete harmony.

人为的音律和雕刻的道理一样,当雕刻的成品出现时,却已经损害到其余的部分,往往失去的更多,只有自然的音律才是完整无缺的。
The principles of music and wood carving are alike — when a wood carving is finished, it has been created at the expense of all the wood that has been carved away. Only the music of nature is complete and undiminished.

丽姬的哭泣
Li Ji's Tears

丽姬做新娘，嫁给晋献公的时候，伤心得把衣服都哭湿透了。
On Li Ji's wedding day, she was to be married to Prince Jin Xian. She was so sad that she drenched her wedding dress in tears.

我不嫁！不嫁！
I'm not marrying him! I won't do it!

后来，到了晋国的王宫，睡在柔软的床上，吃着四海的美味，才知道自己出嫁时，哭泣有多愚蠢。
But after she was married, she found herself sleeping on a long, soft bed and eating food from the four corners of the earth. Who would believe that on her wedding day, she cried her eyes out?

人都怕死，但谁知道死了以后会不会后悔为什么要生？这不正是和丽姬出嫁前后的情形一样吗？
Everyone is afraid of dying, but maybe death will be so great that we'll end up regretting having ever lived.

长梧子的大梦
Zhang Wuzi's Dream

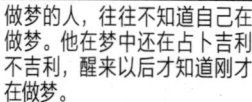

做梦的人，往往不知道自己在做梦。他在梦中还在占卜吉利不吉利，醒来以后才知道刚才在做梦。
A person having a dream is never aware of it, and in his dream he might even do things like predict his own fate. Only after he wakes up does he realize that he was dreaming.

长梧子对瞿鹊说：
Zhang Wuzi said to Ju Que:

有大觉悟的人，才知道生是一场大梦，但有一些愚人，却自以为是大觉悟。
Only the truly enlightened person realizes that life is just one big dream. And then there are those fools who think that they are the enlightened ones.

你在做梦！
You're dreaming!

我和你都在做梦。我说你做梦，也是梦话。
You and I are both dreaming. When I say you are dreaming, that is mere dream talk.

有大疑惑的人，才可能有大觉悟，愚人往往自以为大悟，所以愚人终究还是愚人。
Only those who have great doubts can be truly enlightened. But a fool always believes that he is enlightened, and that is why in the end, he is a fool.

影子的对话
Dialogue With a Shadow

罔两是影子的影子。
Wang Liang is the shadow of a shadow.

喂喂喂
Hey, hey, hey!

你一会儿又走、又停、又坐、又站，干什么？
Would you make up your mind what you want to do! First you walk, then you stop, then you sit, then you stand. I can't take it!

我是有所依赖才会这样子，是不由自主的。
Look, I can't help it, I'm just following him.

蛇靠横鳞才能爬行，蝉靠翅膀才能飞。
A snake depends on its scales to slither, a cicada depends on its wings to fly.

但它们死了，虽有横鳞、翅膀，也仍然不会走、不会飞呀！
But after they die, even though the scales and wings still remain, they can neither slither nor fly.

自然之道是一种变化之道，没有固定的"君"、固定的"臣"。依赖不依赖，才是自然。
Change is a law of nature. There is no designated king or minister. What is natural is deciding whether you are a leader or a follower.

庄周梦见蝴蝶
The Dream of the Butterfly

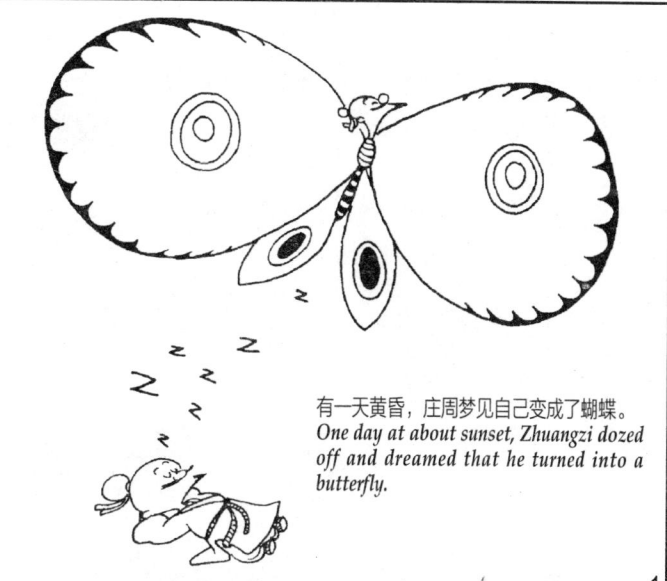

有一天黄昏，庄周梦见自己变成了蝴蝶。
One day at about sunset, Zhuangzi dozed off and dreamed that he turned into a butterfly.

他拍拍翅膀，果然像是一只蝴蝶，快乐极了。这时候，他完全忘记自己是庄周。
He flapped his wings, and, sure enough, he was a butterfly, what a joyful feeling. As he fluttered about, he completely forgot that he was Zhuangzi.

过了一会儿，他在梦中大悟，原来那得意的蝴蝶就是庄周。
Soon, though, he realized that that proud butterfly was in fact Zhuangzi.

那么，究竟是庄周做梦变成蝴蝶？还是蝴蝶做梦变成庄周？
Then, was it Zhuangzi who dreamed that he was a butterfly, or was it a butterfly who dreamed that it was Zhuangzi?

庄周可以是蝴蝶，蝴蝶也可以是庄周。
Maybe Zhuangzi was the butterfly, and maybe the butterfly was Zhuangzi.

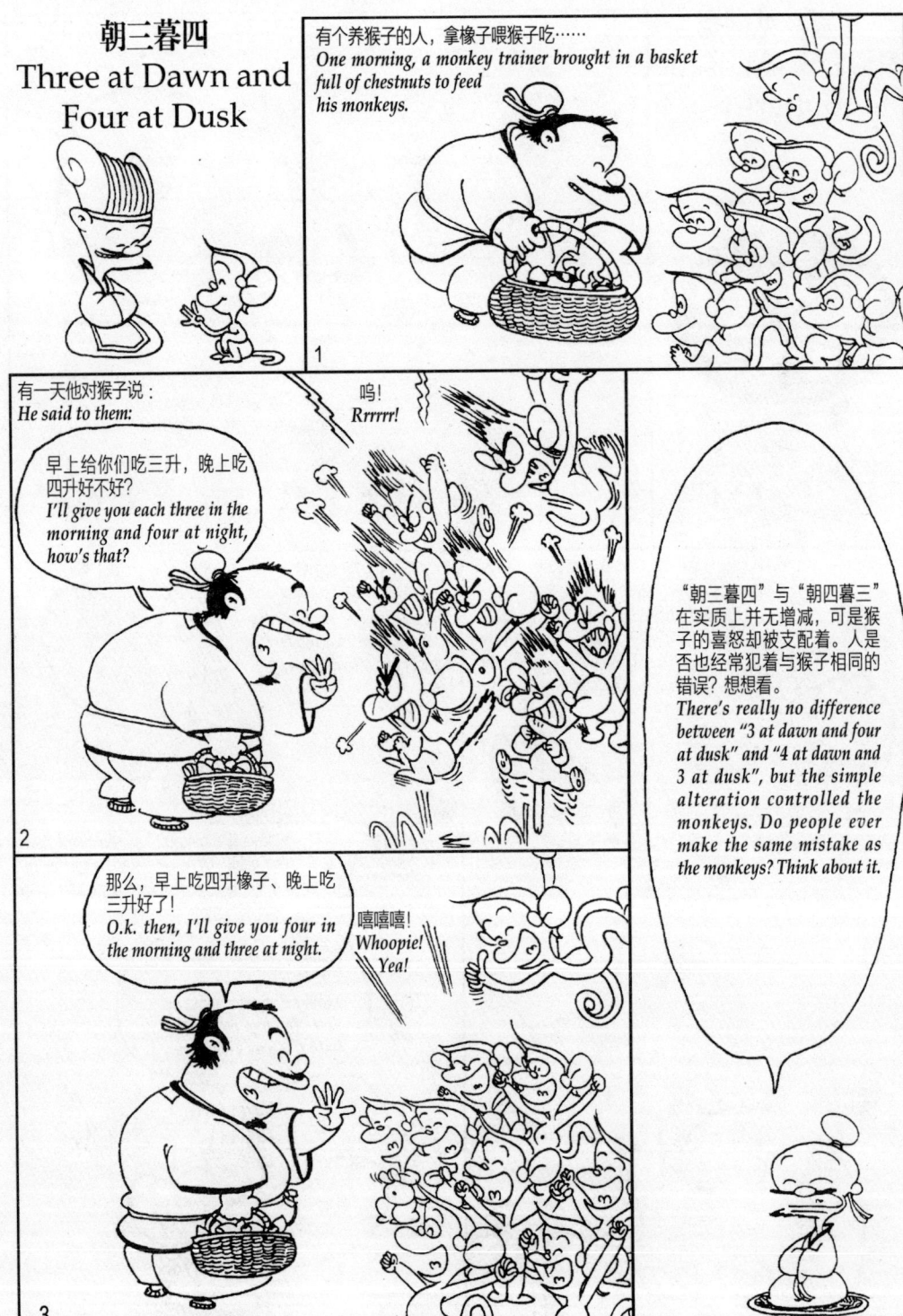

庄子说 自然的箫声

惠施靠在梧桐上
Hui Shi Leans Against a Tree

惠施口才很好，和人辩论了一辈子。
Hui Shi was a man of great rhetorical skills, and he spent his life debating with others.

胜！
Victory!

负！
Defeat.

每当他辩论累了，就靠在梧桐树上休息。
After a hard day's debating, he would prop himself up against a certain tree and rest.

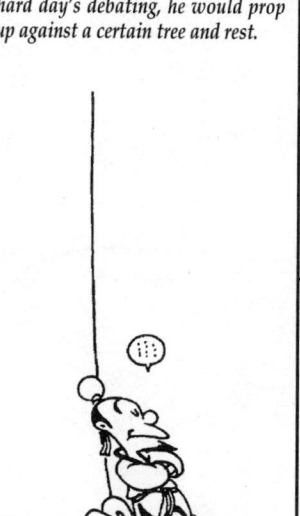

惠施靠在梧桐树上休息的时候，有一次终于悟出了不辩论的道理。
One day, while resting there, he suddenly realized the principle of not debating.

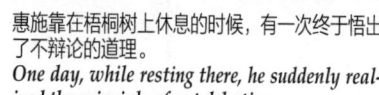

从此就不再劳神去和人家辩论了。
After that he never debated with anyone ever again.

利用口才的辩论，把人驳倒，你便算胜利吗？你认为你"胜利"这正是你的"失败"。
Can relying on rhetoric to defeat someone in a debate really be considered a victory? If you think so, then you've already been defeated.

薪尽火传
Passing on the Flame

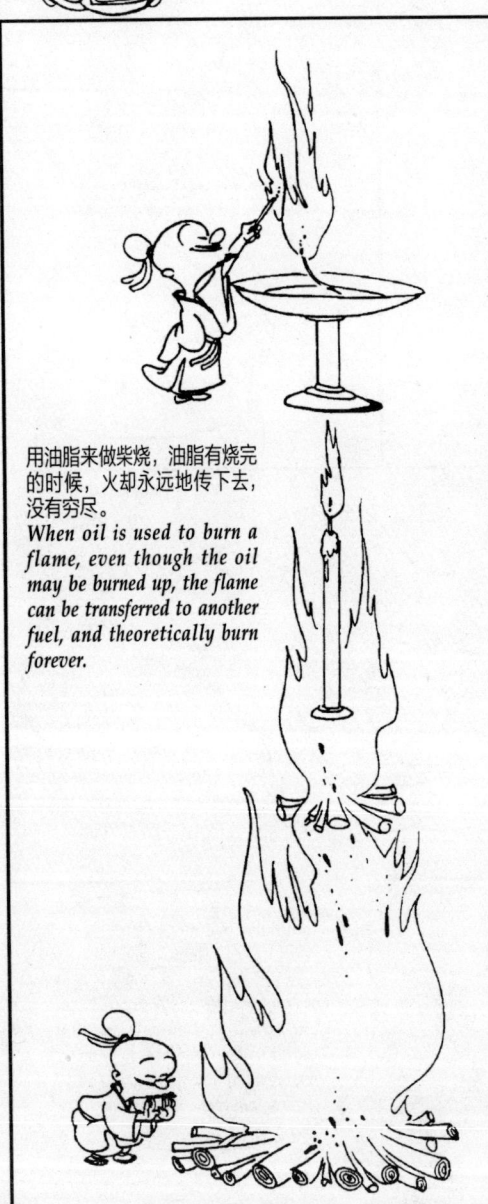

用油脂来做柴烧，油脂有烧完的时候，火却永远地传下去，没有穷尽。
When oil is used to burn a flame, even though the oil may be burned up, the flame can be transferred to another fuel, and theoretically burn forever.

1

道!
Dao!

形体有死亡的一天，但精神、思想却可一再传下去，永远不灭。
Our bodies will die someday, but our spirit and thoughts can be passed on, forever.

道!
Dao!

道!
Dao!

2

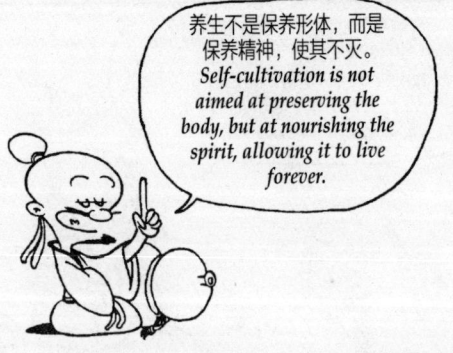

养生不是保养形体，而是保养精神，使其不灭。
Self-cultivation is not aimed at preserving the body, but at nourishing the spirit, allowing it to live forever.

笼中的野鸡
The Caged Chicken

山林中的野鸡求食不易，走十步才找到一条虫。
Finding food isn't easy for the wild pheasant, traveling ten steps before getting a single worm.

走一百步才找到一口水，但它仍不希望被关在笼子里。
And even though it has to walk a hundred paces for a drink of water, it still prefers this to being locked up in a cage.

因为，在笼子里虽然不愁吃喝，羽毛光亮，但精神上终不比在野外自由。
A caged chicken may have enough to eat and drink and it's feathers may be bright and shiny, but it will always crave the freedom of being on the outside.

懂得养生的人，不会因为追求物欲的享受，而付出自由的代价。但在现实的社会里有几个人"头上便是青天"呢？
The person who understands self-cultivation would never pursue material pleasures at the expense of freedom, Yet in today's society, how many truly carefree people do you see?

螳臂当车
The Mantis Stops a Cart

颜阖问蘧伯玉说：
Yan He was about to go on a mission to persuade the evil Prince Fu to change his ways. Before leaving, he went to Qu Boyu for advice:

有个人天性嗜杀，如果放纵了他，便会危害国家。
There is a person who is a killer by nature.

如果去劝他向善，便会先危害到自己。
If left to his own devices, he will bring harm upon the nation. And if one attempts to persuade him otherwise, he will bring harm upon the persuader.

那个人通常只看到人家的过失，看不见自己的过失！
This person sees only the faults of others and is blind to his own shortcomings. What can be done?

对付这种人要善巧和顺，别激怒他。
In dealing with this type of person, you must first be flexible and conform to his behavior. Don't anger him.

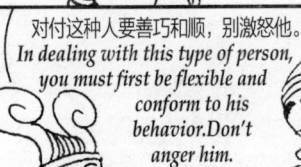

他像婴儿一样，你便也装作婴儿一样。
If he acts like a child, you act like a child.

他颠三倒四，你也装作颠三倒四一样。
If he acts like a lunatic, you act like a lunatic.

哈哈哈 Ha ha ha

不可想象的怪人
The Freak

有一个怪人,头弯到肚脐下面,两个肩膀高过头顶,发髻朝天,五脏不正,腰夹在两股中间,他叫做——支离疏。
There once was a very peculiar man named Zhi Lishu, whose body was terribly deformed. His head was bent down below his navel, shoulders reached up above the top of his head, hair stuck out in all directions, vital organs were all out of place, and stomach was down between his thighs.

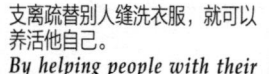

支离疏替别人缝洗衣服,就可以养活他自己。
By helping people with their laundry, Zhi lishu could make enough money to get by.

替人卜卦算命,可以养活十几个人。
And by telling fortunes, he could support a dozen people.

大吉大利
Very lucky, very lucky.

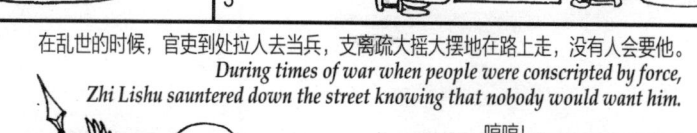

在乱世的时候,官吏到处拉人去当兵,支离疏大摇大摆地在路上走,没有人会要他。
During times of war when people were conscripted by force, Zhi Lishu sauntered down the street knowing that nobody would want him.

哼哼!
Humby dee dum dum.

有时候……政府救济贫民,支离疏列入甲级贫户,可以领到不少的柴米。
During times of famine when the government gave out free grain, Zhi Lishu would be first in line due to his disability.

米 Rice

有智慧的人,不计较形貌的残缺和丑陋。残缺和丑陋也能免除许多祸害。
The wise person doesn't care about an unappealing aspect or disabilities. These attributes can also save one from much grief and hardship.

对!
Right!

没有脚指头的废人
Toeless Shu

鲁国有一个被砍去脚指头的人名叫叔山无趾。
There once was a man in Lu by the name of Toeless Shu Shan. Toeless Shu had had his toes chopped off for committing a crime.

有一天,他用脚跟走路来见孔子。
One day, he walked on his stumps to go see confucius.

从前你不自爱,才被官府砍掉了脚指头。今天就算你来见我也已经太晚了。
It's because you didn't care about you're own well-being that you had your toes cut off. It's too late to change that now.

我的脚趾虽然不见了,但我身上还有比脚趾重要的东西啊,我来见你就是想保全那些更宝贵的东西呀。
I may not have any toes, but the rest of my body is still here, and I came to you in the hope of preserving that.

真是对不起!
I apologize!

请你进门来指导指导我的门徒吧!
You are a wise man. Please come in and teach my disciples.

哼!
Hmph!

叔山无趾是有德之人,所以孔子对他再也不敢怠慢。那么形体的残缺,当然也就不能决定哪个人是废人了。
Toeless Shu Shan was a man of high virtue, and that is why Confucius changed his attitude toward him. A simple disability does not make one a cripple.

叔山无趾不再说话,径自走了。
But Toeless Shu had already started on his way.

自然是超级英雄
Nature the Superhero

自然就像是一位超级英雄，它的无限实力在不断涌动。
Nature is like a superhero, its limitless strength continually pulsing.

自然给予了我身体；
Nature gave me my body;

赐予我活力使得我可以努力工作；
Gave me vitality so that I can work hard;

给予我年龄令我可以安心舒适地老去；
Gave me age so that I can grow old in ease and comfort;

赐予我死亡，令我获得永恒的平静。
Gave me death so that I can have everlasting peace.

自然是不断变化的，人们必须承认，并去适应这些变化。这样你就不会永远处于恐惧和愤怒之中，生命和死亡之间的区别也将失去意义。
Nature is constantly changing, and people have to acknowledge and adapt to these changes. This way you won't always be fearful and angry, and the distinction between life and death will lose its significance.

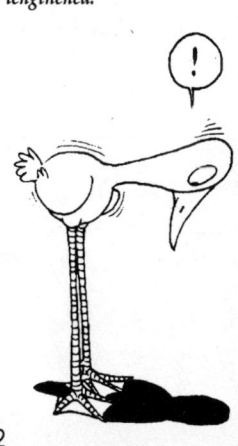

盗亦有道
Thieves Have Principles, Too

1. 盗跖是古代的大盗……
Once upon a time, there was a notorious thief named Dao Zhi.

敢问大王……
Excuse me, I have a question...

2. 我们盗也有"道"吗?
Do we thieves have principles, too?

当然有!
Of course we do!

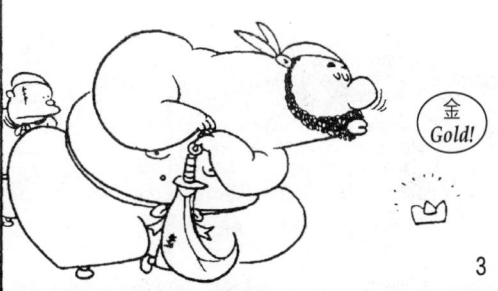

3. 做大盗的人,能预先猜出房间里的财物在哪里,叫做"圣"。
Being able to find out where hidden treasure is, is called Sagacity.

金
Gold!

4. 偷东西的时候,一马当先,叫做"勇"。
When robbing a house, going in first is called Courage.

我先进去探路!
I'll go in first and take a look around.

5. 偷完以后,最后才出来,叫做"义"。
After a robbery, coming out last is called Chivalry.

你们先走,我来断后!
You guys go ahead, I'll take up the rear.

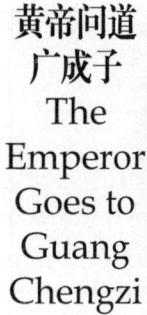

黄帝问道广成子
The Emperor Goes to Guang Chengzi

这时候,他听说广成子已得大道,便亲自上山向广成子问道。
When the emperor had been reigning for nineteen years and had brought peace and prosperity to the land, he heard about an enlightened master named Guang Chengzi.

我想用天地的精气,调合阴阳二气,帮助五谷成熟,我想帮助百姓调养性情……
I want to use the vitality of nature to harmonize the Yin and the Yang, this will bring unprecedented harvests. I want to stabilize the lives of my people...

黄帝在位十九年,教化大行于天下。
Out of curiosity, the emperor went to see him.

你想利用大道的精气助长万物,那反而是摧残它们了。用人的智力去改变人间事,只是揠苗助长而已,难道你不懂吗?
You say you want to use the vitality of the Dao to enhance the natural processes? This will only destroy them. Don't you understand that to use our intellect to change things only makes matters worse?

1　　2

黄帝听了心如死灰,立刻退位,抛了天下,到荒野独居,清清静静地住了三个月……
Upon hearing this, the king's passion turned to dust and he immediately abdicated. He left the world behind and went to live by himself in a grass hut. He stayed there in peace and solitude for three months.

3　　4

我要怎样修身,才能长久?
What can I do to live a long life?

5　6

大道一片浑沌,不明也不暗。
The Dao is chaotic, neither bright nor dark.

你不要用眼睛去看,不要用耳朵去听,不要用心去想,要形神抱元合一,无知无我,要顺应自然、参与自然,合而为一,便可长久。
Don't see with your eyes, Don't hear with your ears, Don't think with your mind, Embrace the primal one, No knowledge, no self, Go with nature, Participate in nature, be one with nature, And a long life will come naturally.

自然的友
Nature's Friend

1. 师法大自然的智慧的至人,他的教化,像……"形体和影子"的关系一样……
There is a kind of sage who emulates the wisdom of nature. His teaching methods are like the relationship of a form and its shadow.

2. 像……"声音和回音"的关系一样。
Where there's a question, there's an answer; where there's and action, there's a reaction.

有问必答,有感必应。
a sound and its echo.

喂 Hello!
喂 Hello!

3. 因为他的形体合一,他停止的时候,没有声音。
Because body and spirit are in harmony. When he is at rest, there is no sound.

4. 他行动的时候,没有痕迹。所以他可以把迷乱的世人,带回自然的大道。
When he moves, he leaves no trace. Therefore, he is able to bring those who are muddled and confused back to the natural Dao.

5. 认为有自我形体的是三代以下的君子。认为没有自我形体的,才是自然的友伴。
Those people who believe that one's body is the temple of one's soul may well enough be good people, but the person who is able to go beyond his corporeal form is the true companion of nature.

6. 无私无我,才合乎自然之道。因为,人的形体,是自然变化中的一种形式而已。如果将其执为己有,那是私心的作用了。
Only the selfless person can live up to the standards of nature because your body is just one temporary form in nature's constantly changing process. Selfishness is trying to hang on to what you have.

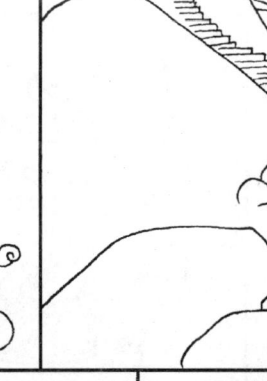

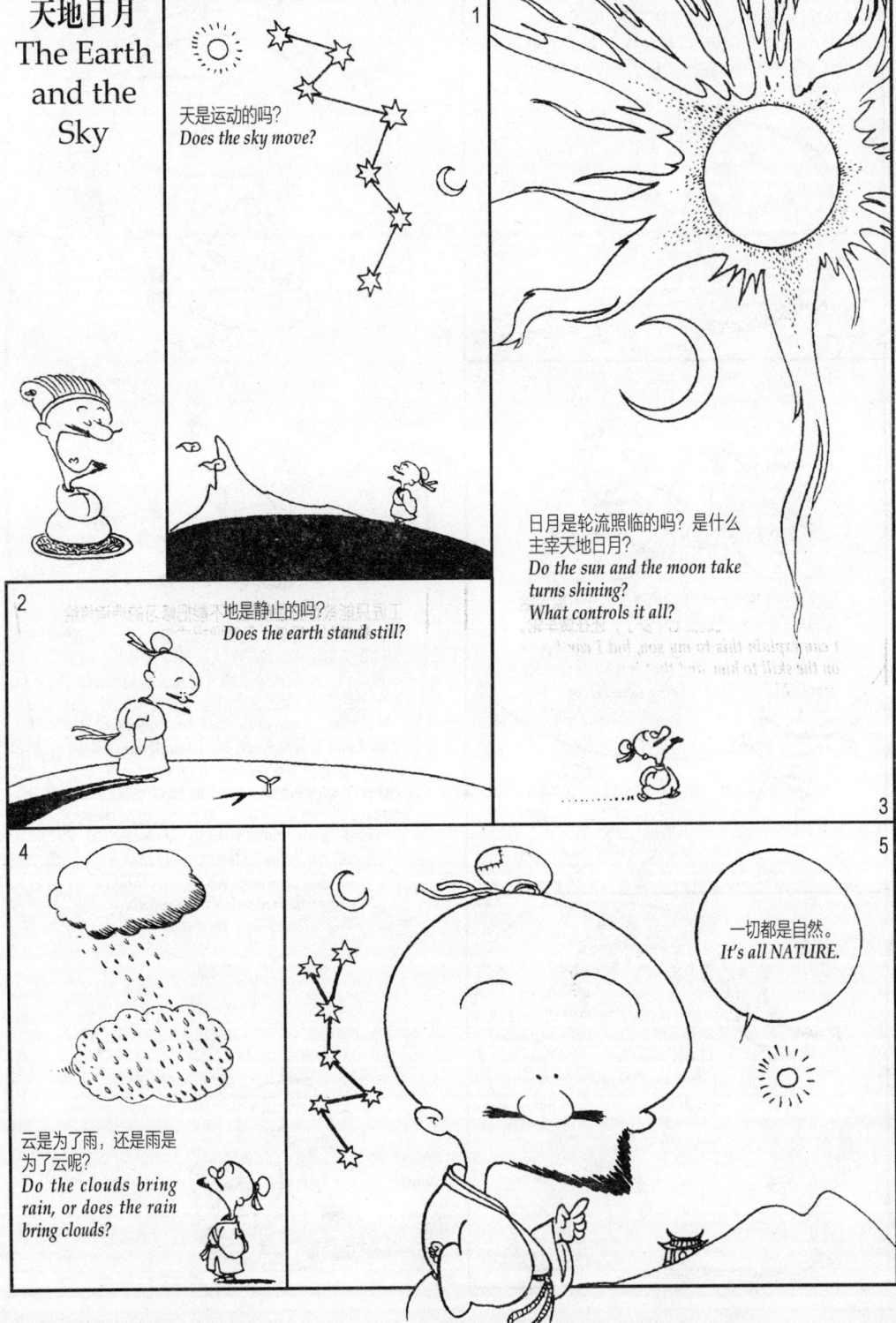

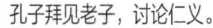

海鸥和乌鸦
Crows and Seagulls

孔子拜见老子，讨论仁义。
One day, Confucius dropped in on Laozi to discuss benevolence and justice.

乌鸦不是天天染黑才黑的。
And crows don't become black by dipping themselves in ink every day.

老子说：海鸥不是天天洗澡才白的。
In the course of the conversation, Laozi said: Seagulls don't become white by washing themselves every day.

黑白都出于自然的本质。所以不能说白比黑好。
Black and white are both natural characteristics. So you can't say one is better than the other.

白的好看！
White is beautiful!

黑的才好看！
Black is beautiful!

无聊！
Gimme a break!

你用仁义去分辨善恶，在懂得大道的人看来，你所犯的错误，和这种道理一样啊！
To a person who understands the Dao, when you use benevolence and justice to distinguish between good and evil, you're making the same mistake.

孔子看到龙
Confucius Sees a Dragon

1. 孔子见了老子，回去三天，不说一句话。
After his meeting with Laozi, Confucius returned home and didn't speak for three days.

2. 老师你去见老聃拿什么去教导他呢？
Master, when you went to see Laozi what did you teach him?

唉唉唉！
Um, um, um!

3. 我看到龙啦，龙顺着阴阳变化无穷。我张着嘴巴，话都说不出来，哪里还谈得上教导他呢？
I saw a dragon, flowing with the Yin and Yang, ceaselessly changing. I opened my mouth, but no sound came out. What could I possibly teach him?

孔子认为老聃已得自然之道，变化无穷。面对一个得道的人，任何的话都是多余、不必要的。
Confucius knew that Laozi understood the way of nature ceaseless transformation. When facing a person who understands the Dao, words are useless and unnecessary.

不要穿牛鼻
Don't Ring the Bull's Nose

1. 河伯问海神说：
One day, Hebo asked the sea spirit:

什么叫自然？什么叫人为？
What is natural and what is man-made?

2. 牛马各有四只脚，这叫自然。
Four legs on horses and cows is natural.

3. 把马头套上辔衔，
A horse's harness,

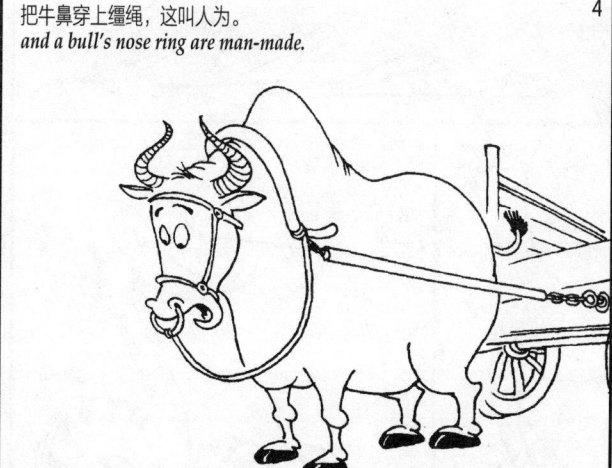

4. 把牛鼻穿上缰绳，这叫人为。
and a bull's nose ring are man-made.

人为的知识、道理、法制，都是违背自然，就像"穿牛鼻络马首"。
Man-made knowledge, morality, and laws all work against nature, just like a horse's harness and a bull's nose ring.

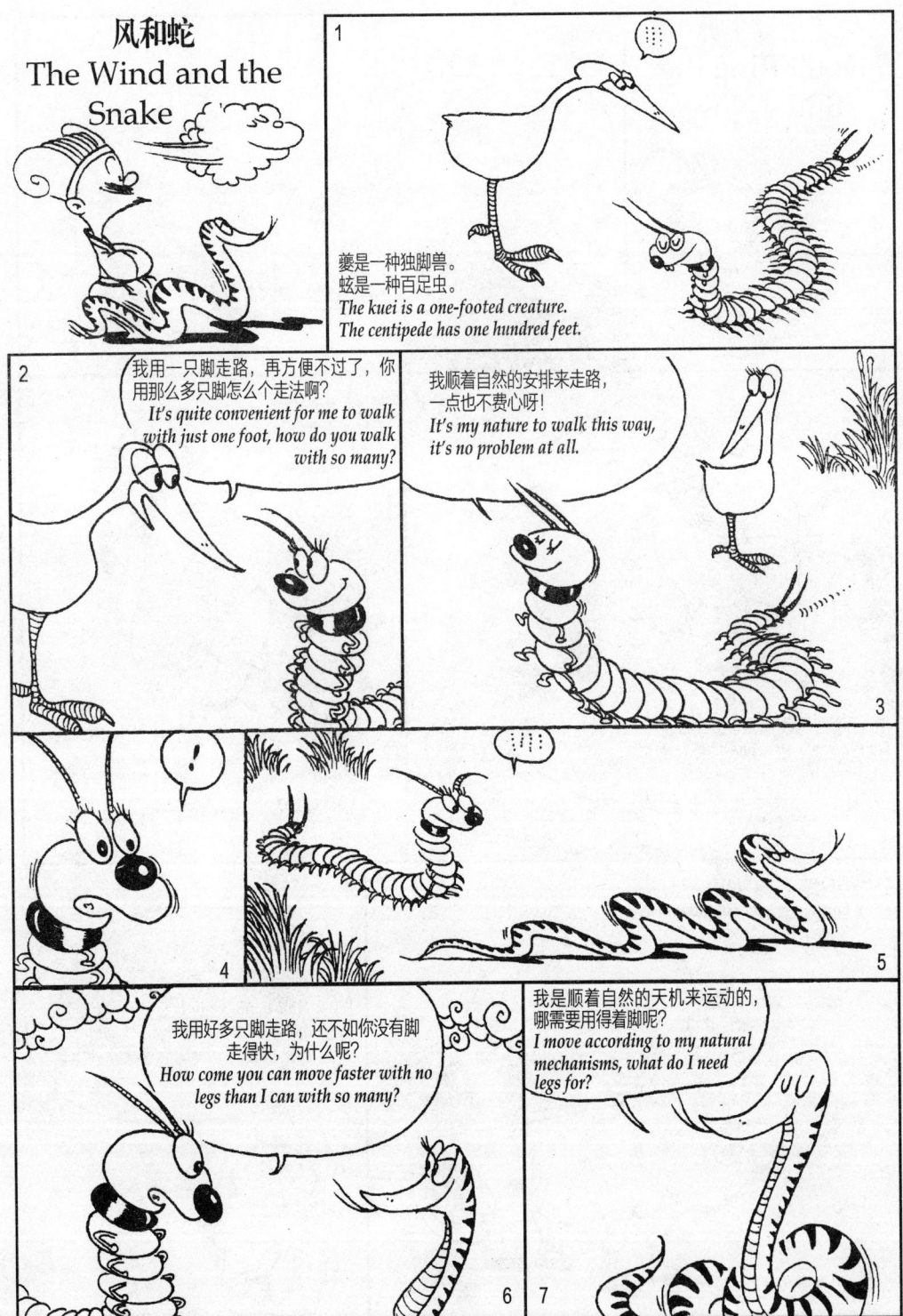

邯郸学步
Learning How to Walk in Handan

燕国的一个小孩，到赵国的都城邯郸去学习邯郸人的步法。
There was once a little boy in Yan who went to the city Handan to learn how to walk like the people there.

但是，他非但没有学会邯郸人的步法，反而把自己原来走路的步法忘掉了。
But not only did he not learn how to walk there, he forgot how to walk altogether!

哇！我不会走路了！
Ah! I can't walk!

因此，他只好爬着回家。
So he had to crawl home.

读书的人原来为了追求大道恢复自然的本性，但是久而久之，就迷失在书城里面，走都走不出来了。
At the outset, people who study are in search of the essence of nature, but after a while, they get lost in the forest of books and can't get out.

庄子说　自然的箫声

酒醉驾车的人
The Drunk Passenger

喝醉酒的人，从车上坠下来，虽然摔得很重，但也不会死。
One day on the way home, a drunk man fell from his carriage. It was a serious fall, but amazingly, the man wasn't hurt.

因为他那时候，已不知道自己是在坐车，也不知道自己正从车上摔下来……
Because at the time, he didn't even know that he was riding in a carriage, let alone know that he had fallen out of one.

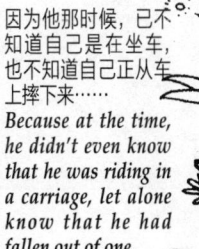

喝醉酒的人就像忘我的人一样，忘我的人，能得自然保护。
Being drunk is just like self-forgetting. If you can forget yourself, then you are safe by nature.

生死惊惧，不能进入他的心中，所以他不会摔死。
Fear of death didn't even enter his mind, so he wasn't hurt.

喂！等等我啊……嘻嘻……
Hey, wait... hiccup!... For me...hiccup!

凡国不曾灭亡
Fan Was Never Destroyed

凡侯和楚王坐着聊天。
A prince from the state of Fan was chatting with the king of Chu when...

凡国灭亡了。
Fan has been conquered!

知道了,退下!
Thank you, that will be all.

是,我的主人!
Yes, my lord.

你心里不急吗?
You're not worried?

我何必急呢?凡国的存在,不能保障自我的存在。凡国的灭亡也不会丧失真我的存在。
What do I have to be worried about? The existence of Fan never guaranteed my existence, and the destruction of Fan will not bring my destruction.

灭亡 destruction
存在 Existence

那么,楚国不正是这样吗?所以,我们不妨说……凡国不曾灭亡,楚国不曾存在。
And the same goes for your country. So we could say that Fan was never destroyed and Chu never existed.

真我才是重要的,外物的存亡变化,哪能时时去计较呢?
What is important is the existence of the self, so why bother complaining about the changes that go on around us?

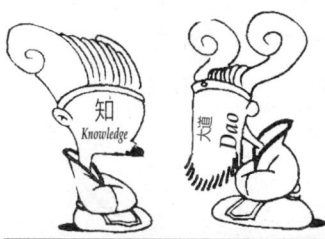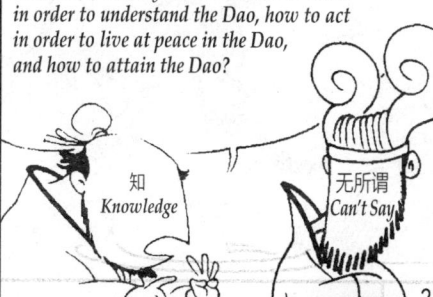

Geng Sangchu Forsakes Fame
庚桑楚逃名

老子的弟子庚桑楚，颇得老子之道。
Geng Sangchu was a very adept student of Laozi.

庚桑楚住在畏垒山上，使畏垒地方的百姓大获丰收。于是当地的人开始感激崇拜他。庚桑楚知道后便对弟子说：
While he was living on a cliff overlooking the village of Wei Lei, harvest time came around and the villagers had a bumper crop. They attributed their good fortune to Geng Sangchu overseeing them and so began to worship and give thanks to him. Geng Sangchu said to his disciples:

春天的时候百草丛生。
In the Springtime, leaves begin to grow and flowers blossom.

秋天的时候万物结果。这是自然的运行啊！我住在这里，人家却把天地的功劳推在我的身上，认为我是贤人，难道我要做人的模范吗？
In the late Summer, plants come to fruition. It's the course of nature! But people say I am responsible for it just because I live up here. They think I am some kind of saint.

于是，他搬到森林里去了。
Thereupon, Geng Sangchu moved away to the forest.

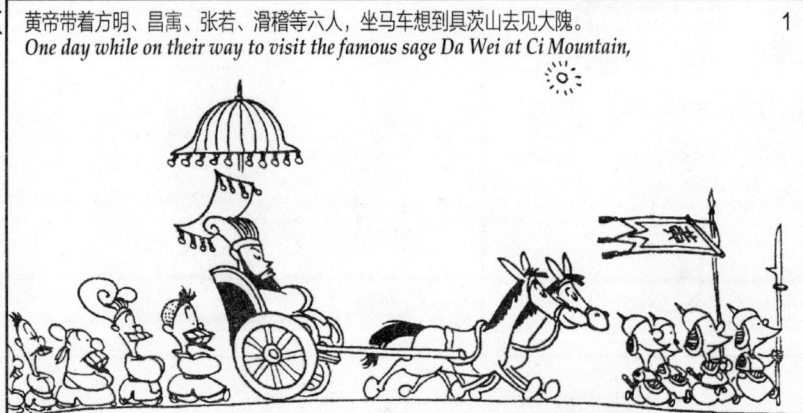

黄帝问道于牧童
The Yellow Emperor and the Pastureboy

黄帝带着方明、昌寓、张若、滑稽等六人，坐马车想到具茨山去见大隗。
One day while on their way to visit the famous sage Da Wei at Ci Mountain,

七圣在路上都迷路了。
The Yellow Emperor and his cortege of advisors lost their way.

你知道具茨山在哪里吗？
Excuse me, do you know the way to Ci Mountain?

知道啊！
Yes, I do.

你知道大隗在哪里吗？
Do you know how to get to the residence of one Da Wei.

知道啊！
Yes, I do.

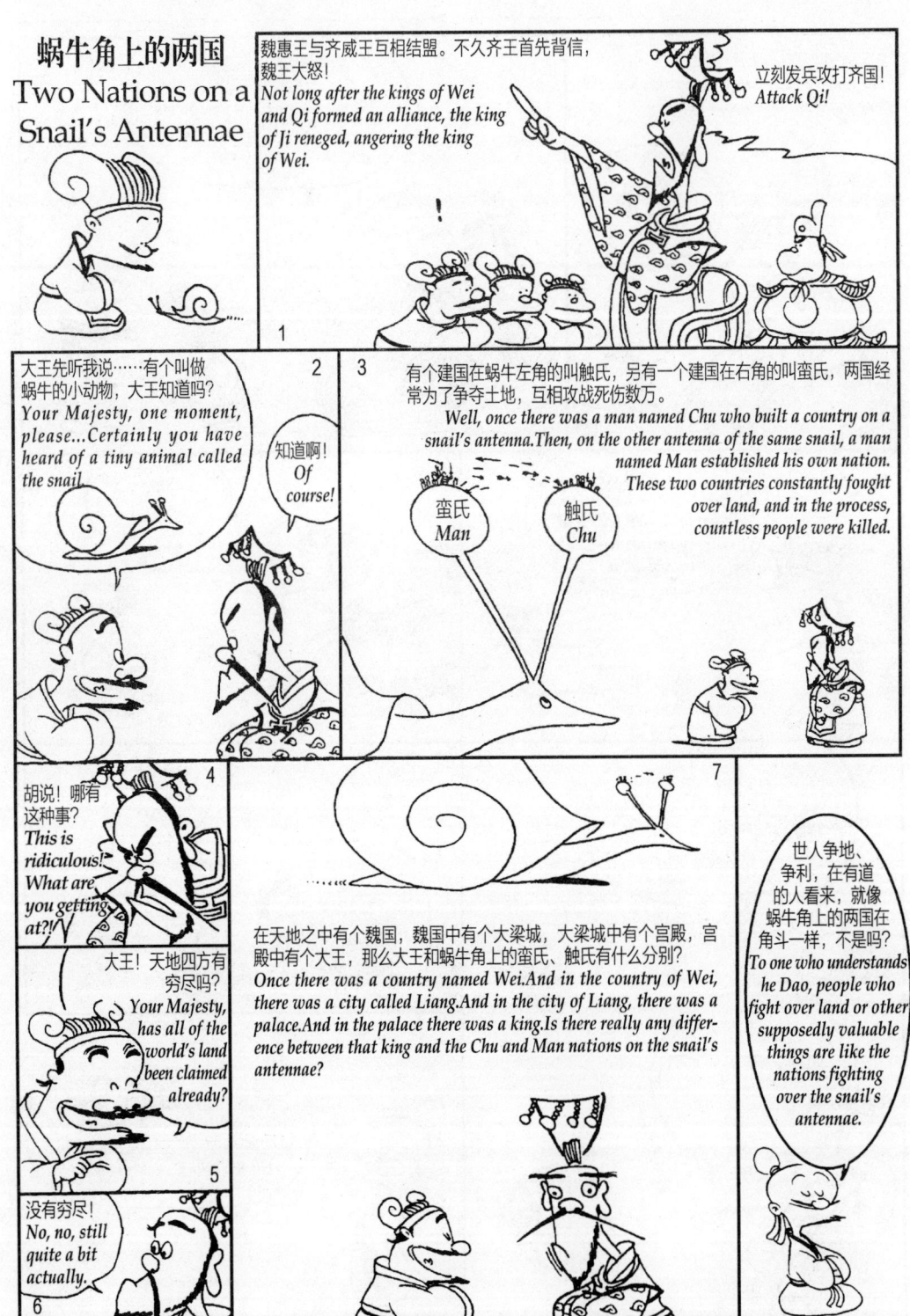

灵验的白龟
The Turtle That Could Predict the Future

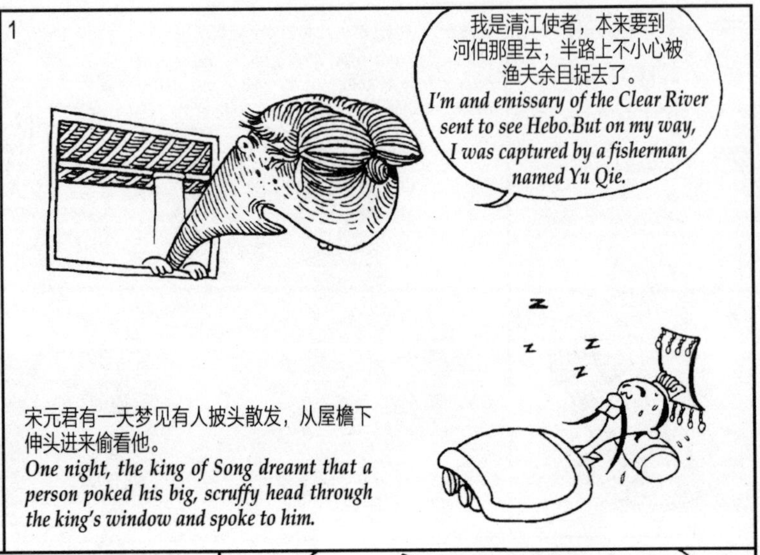

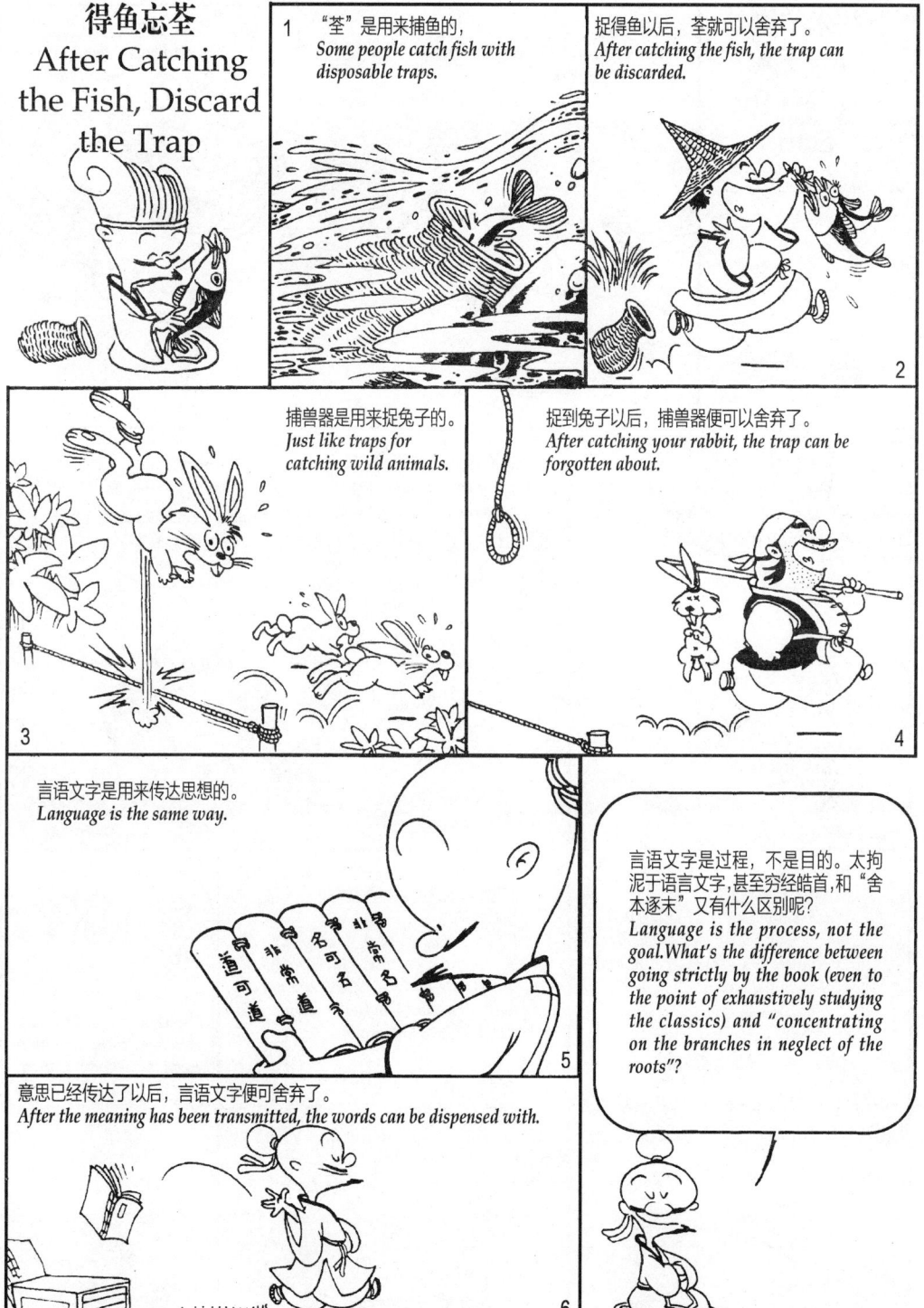

庄子说　自然的箫声

子贡衣服雪白
Zi Gong's Snow White Clothes

原宪和子贡是孔子的学生。
Yuan Xian and Zi Gong were students of Confucius.

原宪家徒四壁，屋顶会漏雨……
Yuan Xian was very poor. He lived in a house where the roof leaked...

门户有漏洞，但他都不在意。
And there was a big hole in one of the walls. But he didn't mind.

子贡很会说话，做了大官，往来很神气。有一天子贡去看原宪。
Zi Gong was a wealthy government official, and one day he paid a visit to Yuan Xian.

巷子太小了，车子开不进去！
The lane is too narrow, sir. The carriage won't fit.

大盗的大道理
The Villain Speaks

柳下季是孔子的朋友，他有个弟弟叫作盗跖。盗跖有部众九千人，横行天下！
Liu Xiaji was a friend of Confucius and had a little brother named Dao Zhi. Dao Zhi had nine thousand followers and together, they ravaged the land.

做父母的要管教儿子，做哥哥的要管教弟弟，现在你弟弟做大盗，横行天下，你不能管管他吗？
Parents should teach their children and older brothers should teach their younger brothers. Your little brother is a terrible villain and ravages the land. Isn't there anything you can do?

有的人就是不听父兄的管教，那又有什么办法？
What can I do? Some people just don't listen.

那就让我去劝劝他吧！
Well, then let me have a try!

我那弟弟个性强悍，如果你拂逆他，他就勃然大怒，我看你还是不要去尝试吧！
Look, my brother has a bad temper. If you cross him, I can't say what might happen. I think it would be better if you didn't go.

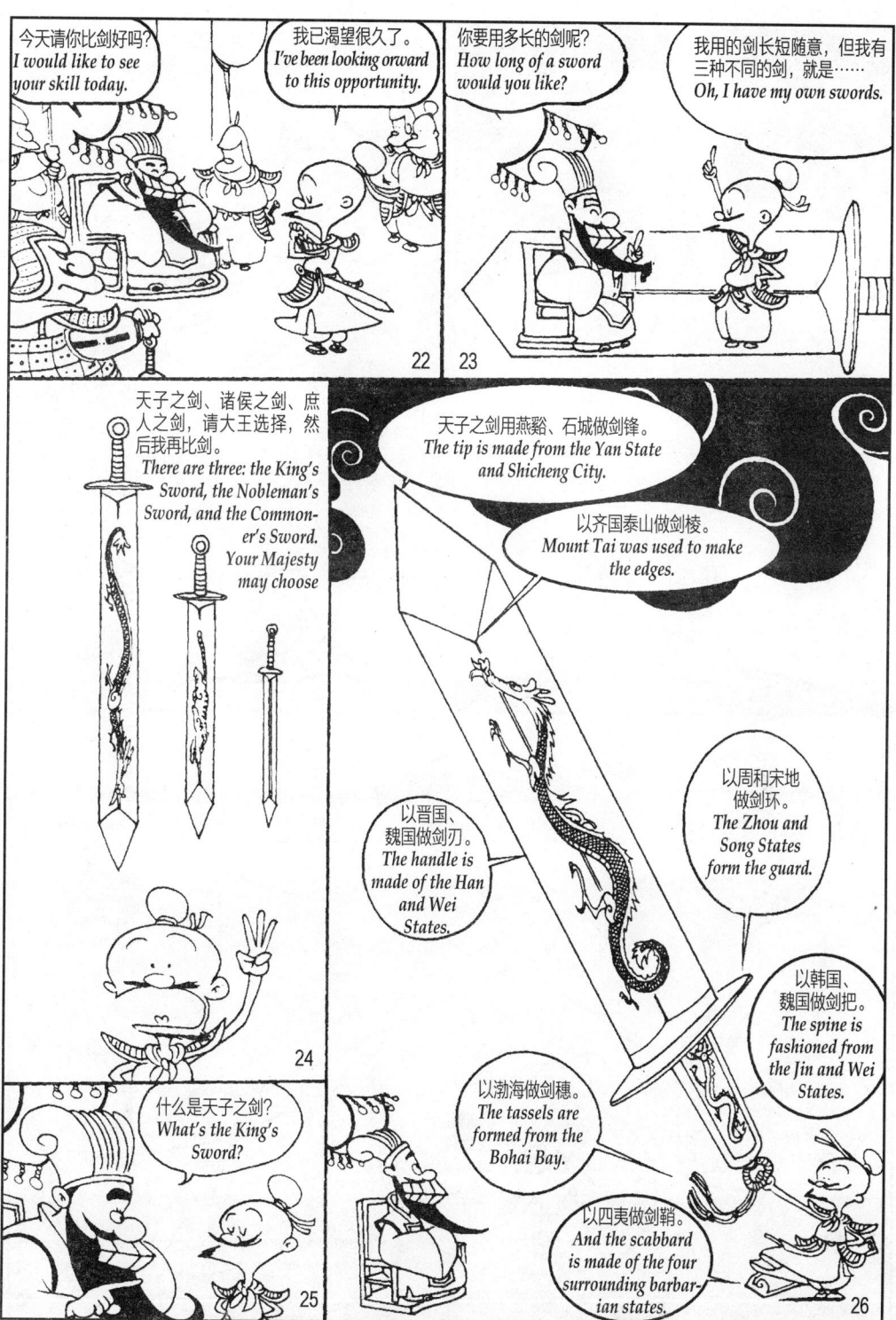

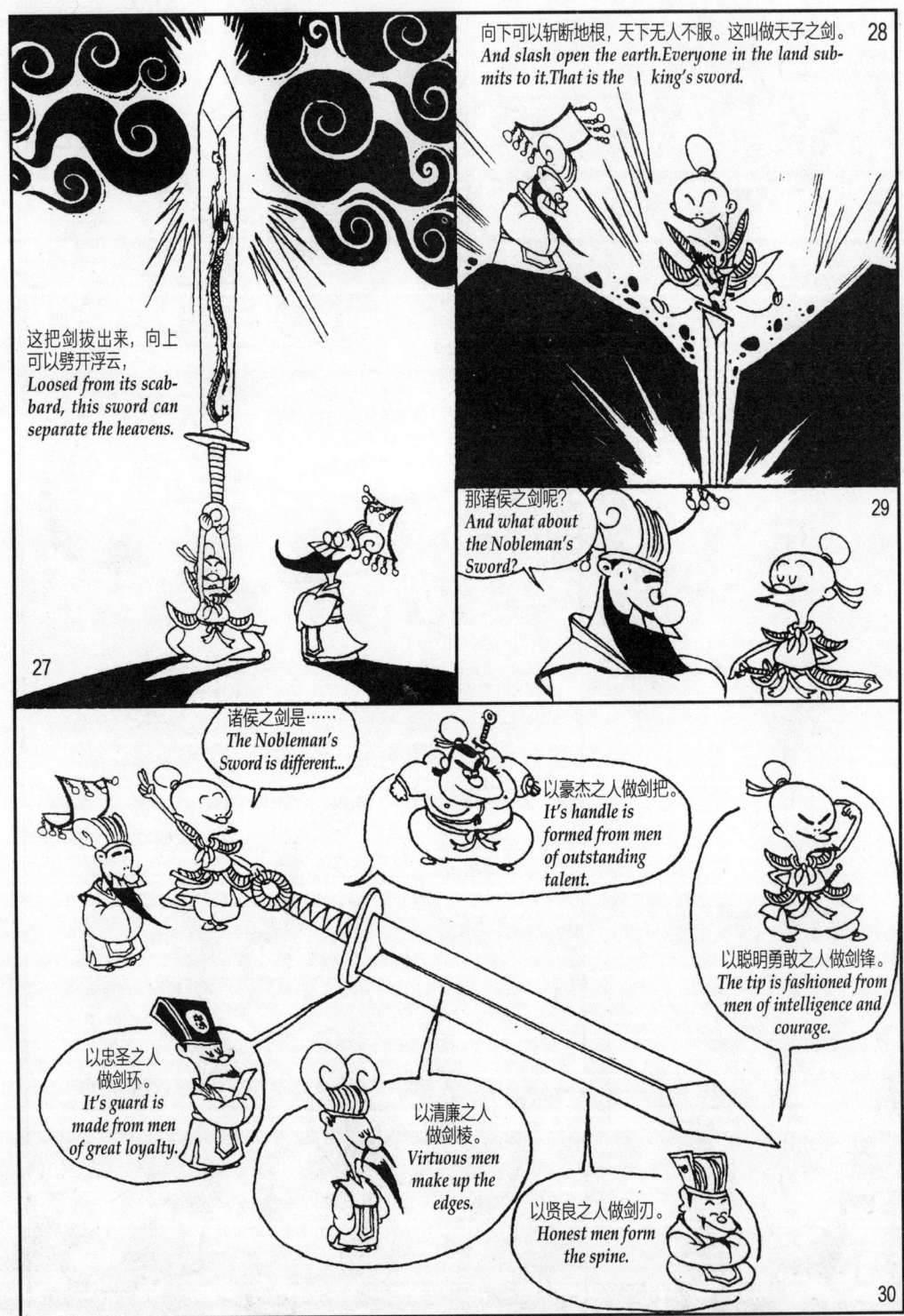

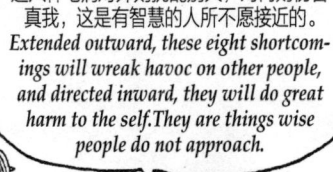

这八种毛病对外则扰乱别人，对内则伤害真我，这是有智慧的人所不愿接近的。
Extended outward, these eight shortcomings will wreak havoc on other people, and directed inward, they will do great harm to the self. They are things wise people do not approach.

好做大事以求功名，这叫做："叨"。
妄作聪明擅自行事，只用自己的主意，不顾侵犯人家的，这叫做："贪"。
看出自己的过失而不改，听了别人的劝谏反而火上加油，这叫做："狠"。
和自己意见相同的，就认为对，和自己意见不同虽好也说不好，这叫做："矜"。
To seek fame through great deeds is called: Ostentation.
To act with reckless disregard for others, selfishly carrying out your own plans is called: Avarice.
To see your own mistakes but not change; to hear other people's good advice but not act on it is called: Malevolence.
To call right those opinions in agreement with yours and call wrong those opinions not in agreement with yours even though they may be good is called: Arrogance.

那么什么是四种忧患呢？
And what are the four failings?

一个人有这四种忧患时，就很难和他谈大道了。
It's difficult to talk about the Dao with one who possesses these four failings.

修大智慧不要犯八病：摠、佞、谄、谀、佚、贼、慝、险。不要犯四患：叨、贪、狠、矜。这八病四患是世人最常见的过失。
If you want to attain great wisdom, don't be guilty of the eight shortcomings: intemperance, obsequiousness, flattery, coquetry, calumniation, craftiness, perfidy, and duplicity. And don't be caught with the four failings: ostentation, avarice, malevolence, and arrogance. These eight shortcomings and four failings are the mistakes most often committed.

孔子听了愀然变色，再三拜揖而去。
Confucius' face turned pale and he bowed three times before departing.

讨厌影子的人
The Man Who Hated His Shadow

有一个人，他讨厌自己的影子。
Once there was a man who hated his own shadow.

讨厌！讨厌！走开！
I hate you! I hate you! I hate you!

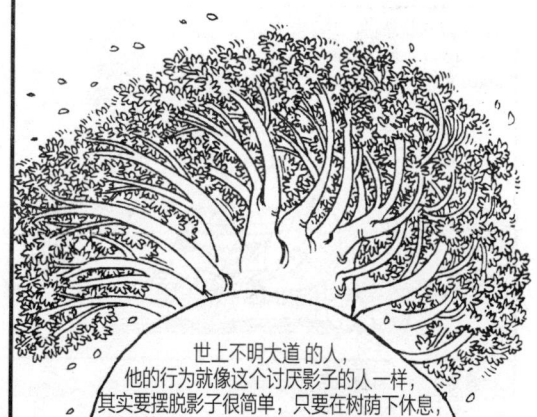

世上不明大道的人，他的行为就像这个讨厌影子的人一样，其实要摆脱影子很简单，只要在树荫下休息，影子就没了。世上人多在狂奔而不肯休息，这是为什么呢？
Those people who don't understand the Dao are just like the man who hated his shadow. It's actually very easy to get rid of your shadow, just rest under a tree, and your shadow disappears. But all those folks running around like crazy people refuse to stop and rest. What do you call that?

当他走路的时候，看见影子紧跟在后便越走越快。但是他走得越快，影子也追得越紧，便发足狂奔，最后……竟累死了。
When he walked and found that his shadow was close behind him, he began to walk faster and faster. But the faster he moved, the closer his shadow came. So he ran like a madman...and in the end, he dropped dead.

泛若不系之舟
Like a Drifting Boat

1

巧妙的人多劳苦。
Talented people have so much work to do.

2

聪明的人多忧愁。
Intelligent people have so much to worry about.

3

无能的人无所求，吃饱了便到处逍遥。
Incompetent people, however, go about in a dreamy bliss, satisfied with enough to eat.

4

好像是一条没有绳索系住的空船，在水面上摇呀摇的自由自在。
Like an unmoored boat, drifting on the water, rocking gently back and forth, carefree and at ease.

聪明巧妙往往带来无穷的累赘。这些系累世人常不自觉。
People of ability and intelligence are constantly distressed, while the general population carries on oblivious to it all.

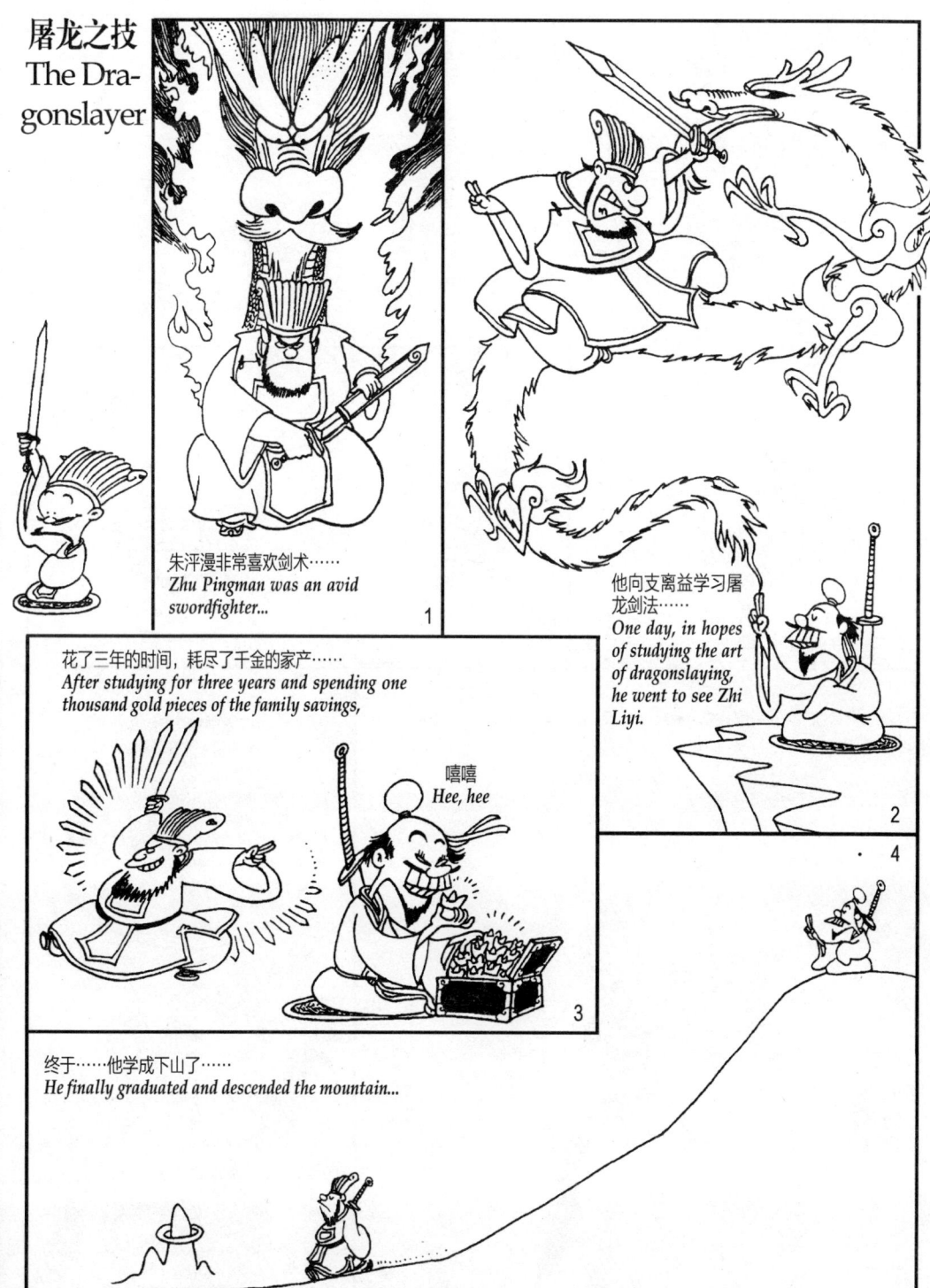

庄子快死了
Zhuangzi on His Deathbed

1 庄子快要死了，他的弟子聚在一起商量，准备厚葬他。
When Zhuangzi was on his deathbed, his disciples gathered around to discuss his burial.

2 那又何必呢？我死后，用天地做棺椁，用日月做双璧，用星辰做珍珠，用万物做礼品，还有什么葬仪比这更好的呢？
Why bother? After I die, use heaven and earth as my coffin; use the sun and moon as burial jades, the stars as jewels, and everything else around me as ritual wares. What funeral could be better than that?

3 这样做，老师会被乌鸦、老鹰吃掉啊！
But, Master, the crows and vultures will get you.

在地上会被乌鸦、老鹰吃掉。在地下，会被蛄蝼、蚂蚁吃掉。你们为什么要把我从乌鸦老鹰的嘴里抢过来给蛄蝼蚂蚁吃呢？
Above ground, the crows and vultures will get me. Below ground, the worms and ants will get me. Why do you insist on taking food out of the mouths of crows and vultures and giving it to worms and ants?

死亡是一种自然肉体的消散、变化就交给大自然去处理吧！
Death is a natural dispersion of the body, so why not give the changes to nature to handle?

庄子说·自然的箫声
（下篇）

Zhuangzi Speaks II
More Music of Nature

蔡志忠　漫画中国传统文化经典

庄子
Zhuangzi

谁是主宰
Who's the Master?

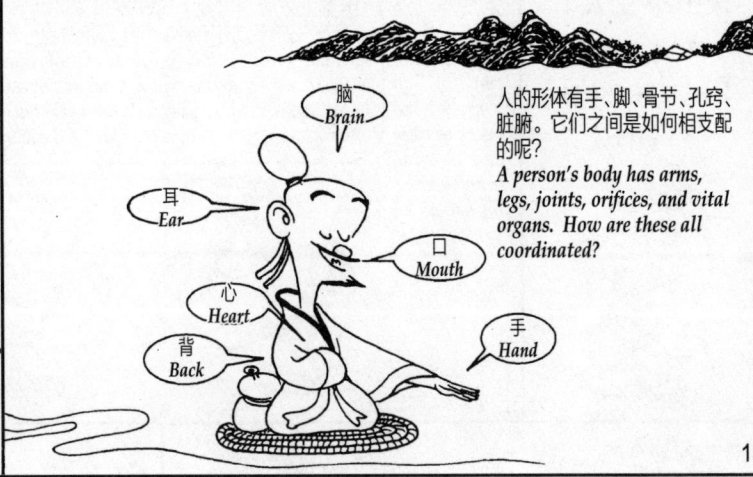

脑 Brain
耳 Ear
口 Mouth
心 Heart
背 Back
手 Hand

人的形体有手、脚、骨节、孔窍、脏腑。它们之间是如何相支配的呢?
A person's body has arms, legs, joints, orifices, and vital organs. How are these all coordinated?

1

它们都是奴婢来服侍我吗?
奴婢怎能互相支配?
Are they all there to serve me?
How can servants be coordinated?

2

是奴婢互相轮流支配吗?
还是另有真正的主宰呢?
Do they take turns coordinating each other?
Or is there a genuine master that controls them all?

3

事实是形体之外尚有精神,这个精神就是真正的主宰啊!
Whether or not we come to know this master will not alter its genuineness one way or the other.

4

人都具有自己的"实有的真心",这个实有的真心乃是大自然的道的缩影。人能以此为法则,去发展一切的行动,自不离自然的正道。
Everyone has their own genuine mind, which is a miniature of the natural Dao. So if you can act in accordance with it, you will never be far from the Dao.

养生主
The Danger of Knowledge

人的生命有限，知识却是无穷。
A lifetime is limited, but knowledge is limitless.

1

如果以有限的生命，去追求无穷的知识，那是非常危险的。
To take a limited life and pursue limitless knowledge can be very hazardous.

2

3

4

知道危险，却以为知识使你聪明，那就更危险了。
To know it is hazardous and still think that knowledge makes you smarter is even more dangerous.

人要超越知识，而不是背负知识，为知识所累。知识是了解养生的道理，了解后，便顺应自然的变化，不要再追逐多余的知识。
We should transcend knowledge, rather than be burdened or tied down by it. Knowledge is used in understanding the principles of nurturing life, but once we understand, we should just follow the natural transformations and not pursue superfluous knowledge.

庄子说 自然的箫声

秦失不哭泣
Qin Shi Didn't Cry

老子死了，秦失来吊丧，哭了几声，就走了。
After Laozi died, Qin Shi went to pay his respects. He let out a few sniffles and then left.

哦?
Oh?

你不是我老师的朋友吗?这样子吊唁可以吗?
Hey, aren't you a friend of the master's? Is that an appropriate way to pay your respects?

老子该来的时候来，应时而生；该走的时候走，顺理而死。安心适时而顺应变化，所以我不必为他悲伤。
Laozi was born when it was time for him to come into the world, and he died when it was time to leave. If you let things happen and abide in the natural changes, you needn't feel any grief.

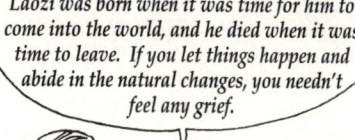

我这样哭哭就可以了。
A few sniffles is just right.

老子的弟子听了，便不再悲伤哭泣了。
Upon hearing this, Laozi's disciples stopped their sorrowful crying.

老子之死，只是形体的死亡，不是精神的死亡。秦失明白这道理，所以不会为他悲伤。
By accepting the transformations of nature, we free ourselves from the bondage of capricious emotions. Qin Shi understood this, and that's why he didn't grieve over Laozi.

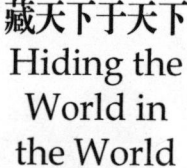

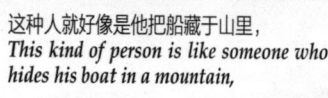

庄子说　自然的箫声

至人用心若镜
The Mind is Like a Mirror

1　绝弃求名的心思；
　　绝弃策谋的智虑；
　　绝弃专断的行为；
　　绝弃智巧的作为。
Do not pursue fame,
Do not occupy yourself with scheming,
Do not concern yourself with trifles,
Do not strive for great wisdom.

2　体会无穷的大道，游心于寂静的境域，承受自然的本性，不自我矜夸，而达到空明的心境。
Experience the boundless and wander in infinity. Use what heaven has given you without boasting about achievements. Just be empty.

3　至人的用心有如镜子，任物的来去而不加迎送……
The perfect person's mind is like a mirror, accepting things as they come and go, neither welcoming them in, nor showing them out.

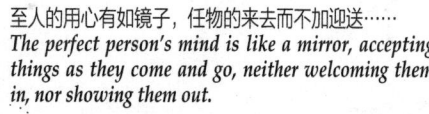

如实反映而无所隐藏，所以能够胜物而不被物所损伤。
And he responds to things naturally without storing them up. Therefore, he is able to overcome material things and not be harmed by them.

至人把心当成镜子，事情来了完全反映，事情去了把心又成空。真切地品尝每一分每一秒。
The perfect person treats the mind like a mirror. When something happens, he responds, and when its over, he empties his mind of it. He genuinely appreciates every moment of life.

4

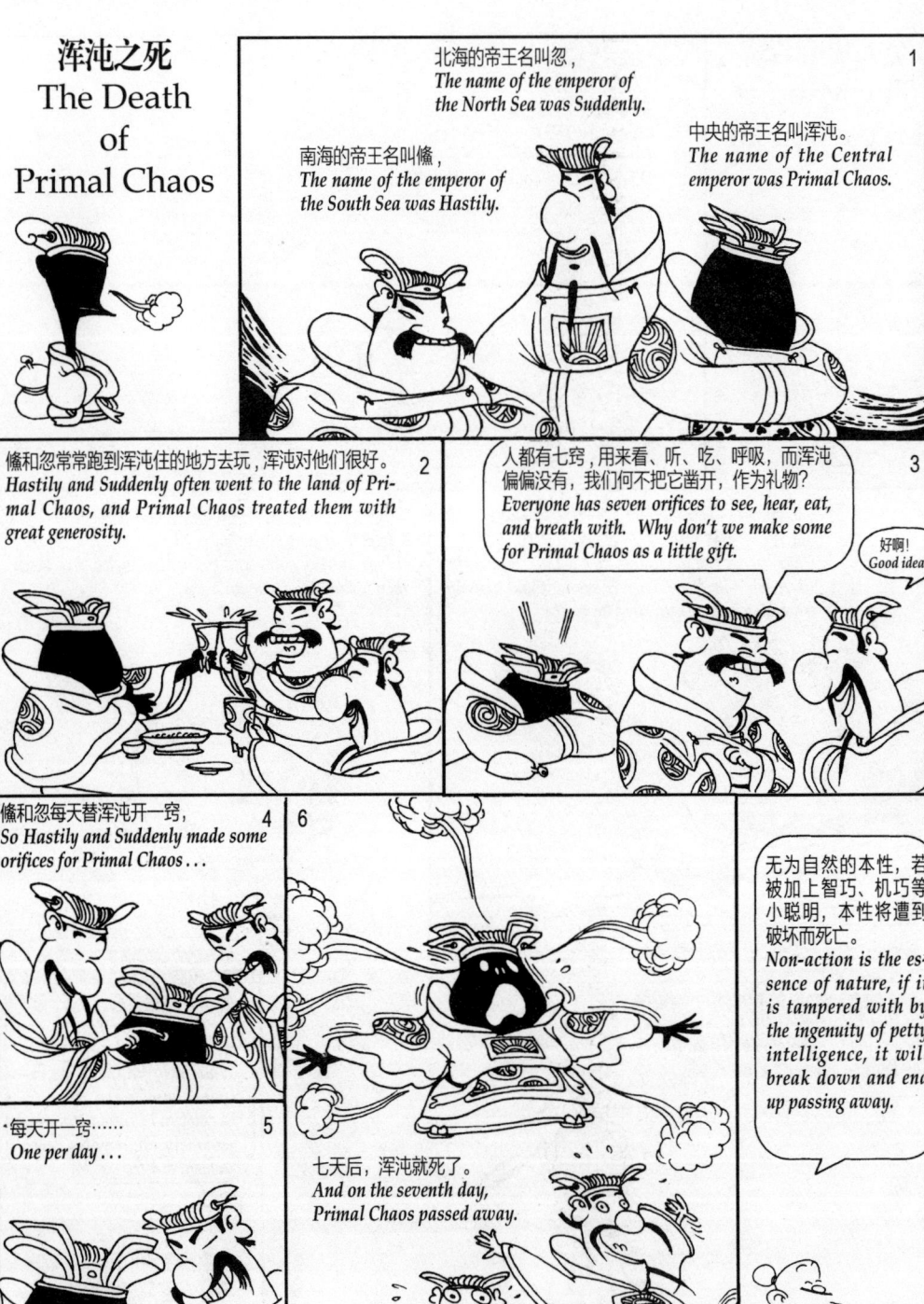

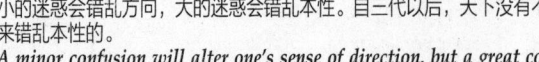

大惑易性
Great Confusion Alters One's Nature

小的迷惑会错乱方向，大的迷惑会错乱本性。自三代以后，天下没有不用外物来错乱本性的。
A minor confusion will alter one's sense of direction, but a great confusion will alter one's original nature. Since the Three Dynasties period, there has been no one who didn't alter their original nature with external things.

小人牺牲自己来求利；
Petty people sacrifice themselves for profit;

名算老几？利才是最实惠的东西。
Fame is for the birds. Profit is what counts.

士人牺牲自己来求名；
Officials sacrifice themselves for fame;

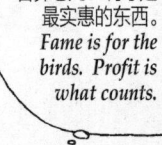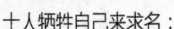

大夫牺牲自己来为家；
Noblemen sacrifice themselves for family;

为了国为了家，生命不足惜。
For my country and my family, life is not to be cherished.

圣人则牺牲自己来为天下。
And sages sacrifice themselves for the whole land.

这几种人，事业不同，名号各异，但是伤害本性、牺牲自己却是一样的，都是迷惑。
These people are all different, with different titles and different stations in life, but their harming their original natures and sacrificing themselves is the same. They are all confused.

5. 他烧铁来烙马，修剪马毛，铲削马掌，在马身上烙印。
They use hot metal to make the coats glisten, clip the manes, trim the hooves, and brand them.

6. 这样一来，马已经死掉十之二三了。
Treated this way, two or three out of ten horses die.

7. 然后为了训练马的耐力，用饥、渴来磨炼它。
Then they train them for endurance, disciplining them through hunger and thirst.

8. 为了调整马的速度，便时快时慢地控制它，用鞭子来催促它。
They use a whip to control the speed, alternating between fast and slow …

9. 马受了这些折磨以后，又关在马厩里，失去了自由，马就死去一大半了。
After these tortures and being shut up in a stable and losing their freedom, half of all horses will die.

无心作为，人民自然感化；清静不扰，人民自然正当。圣人治人，矫造礼乐仁义，于是虚伪狡诈也跟着出现了。
Through non-intentional action, the people are naturally transformed. Through tranquillity and non-interference, the people are naturally upright. A sage tries to govern by contriving propriety, music, righteousness, and benevolence, and with them, hypocrisy and deceit arise.

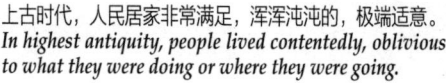

仁义之害
The Harm of Benevolence and Righteousness

1. 上古时代，人民居家非常满足，浑浑沌沌的，极端适意。
In highest antiquity, people lived contentedly, oblivious to what they were doing or where they were going.

2. 随随便便的，挺胸叠肚四出游。
Completely at ease, they walked around with protruding bellies and wandered where they would.

3. 后来圣人矫造礼乐，来匡正天下人的形体，用仁义来教化天下人的心性；
Then sages came along contriving propriety and music to rectify people's appearances and postulating benevolence and righteousness to transform their original natures.

4. 于是，人民就开始矜夸自己，欺诈别人，竞争利益，无法禁止。
From then on, people began boasting of themselves, deceiving others, and contending for advantages, all in an unstoppable wave.

大道废，有仁义；智慧出，有大伪；上古的时候，人民诚实，不识不知，根本没有虚伪，何必需要仁义呢？
With the destruction of the Dao, benevolence and righteousness arise. With the coming of intelligence, deception and hypocrisy arise. In highest antiquity, people were ignorant yet honest. They didn't even know what deception and hypocrisy were, so why would they need benevolence and righteousness?

黄帝遗失玄珠
The Lost Pearl

1 黄帝来到赤水之北，登上昆仑山去游玩。
One day, the Yellow Emperor traveled north of the Chi river and ascended a slope of the Kunlun mountains.

2 返回时，遗失了大道……
On his way back, he lost his mysterious pearl...

3 他令智慧去寻，却找不着。
He ordered Knowledge to go look for it, but he couldn't find it.

4 让离朱用眼睛寻找，也找不到……
Then he sent Li Zhu to look for it with his keen eyes, but he couldn't find it.

庄子说　自然的箫声

无江海而闲
Independent Leisure

1. 刻意高尚自己的行为，表示和世俗不同；议论唱高调，抨社会的黑暗，表示心中的不平，这是愤世嫉俗的人的做法。
Curbing ambition and praising conduct, seeing oneself as special and separate from the world, sermonizing and bemoaning the evils of the world—these are but for the sake of something higher and are what forest hermits, cynics, and idealists like to do.

2. 提倡忠信仁义，恭俭推让，以便修养自己或教诲别人，这是游历各地，或在固定地方讲学的人的做法。
Speaking of benevolence, righteousness, conscientiousness, and trustworthiness, respecting frugality, and promoting humility—these are but for the sake of self-cultivation and are what political hopefuls, instructors, and itinerant scholars like to do.

3. 讲大功、立大名，定君臣上下的礼节，以治平天下。这是富国强兵，兼并土地的人的做法。
Speaking of great accomplishments, establishing great reputations, maintaining the sovereign-vassal relationship, and rectifying the superior-inferior relationships—these are but for the sake of governing and are what court patrons, citizens of superpowers, and aggressors like to do.

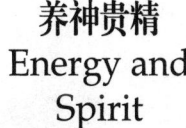

养神贵精
Energy and Spirit

1. 形体劳苦不休息，就会累坏……
If the body toils without rest, it will become fatigued...

2. 精力用之不已，就会疲劳枯竭……
If one's energy is used without a break, it will be exhausted...

譬如水的本性，不混杂它就清，不搅动它就平……
For instance, it is the nature of water to be pure when it is not made turbid, to be calm when it is not stirred up...

但若闭塞不流动，它又会浊而不清。这种静静地随着自然的运用就是自然现象。
If it is blocked up and unable to flow, it cannot be pure. This is a natural phenomenon.

3.

4.

所以说纯粹不杂，虚静专一而不变动，淡泊无为，举动都顺着天然，就是养神之道。
So it is said that purity without turbidity, tranquillity without alteration, simplicity without action, movement with the natural way are all the Dao of nurturing the spirit.

精神如同干将莫邪宝剑，藏在柜里不可轻易动用。
The spirit is like a precious sword. It should be kept in a case and not imprudently removed.

普通人重利，廉洁的人重名，贤人高尚意志，圣人宝贵精神！
Common people emphasize profit, upright people emphasize reputation, worthies praise ambition, and sages cherish the spirit!

5.

6.

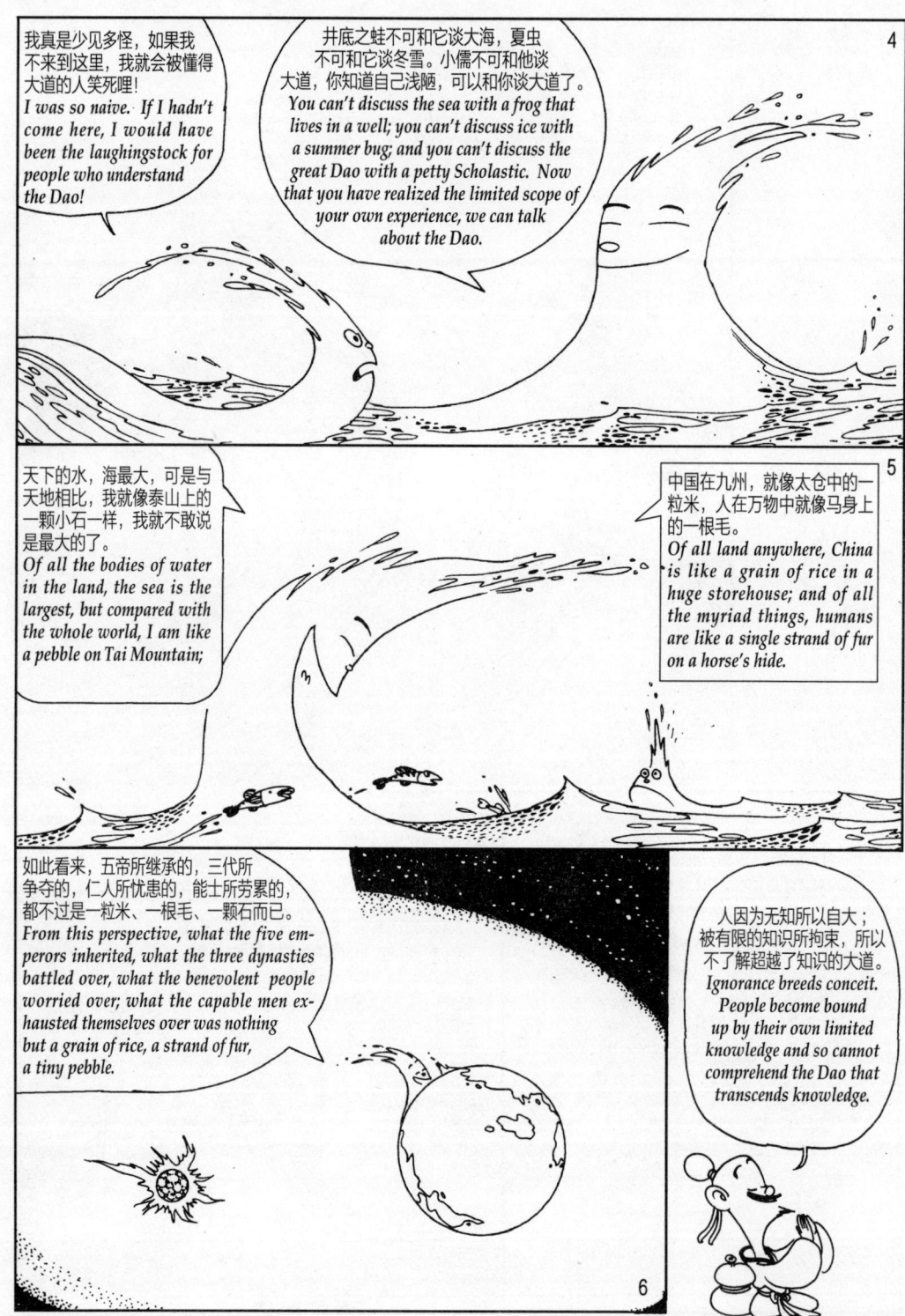

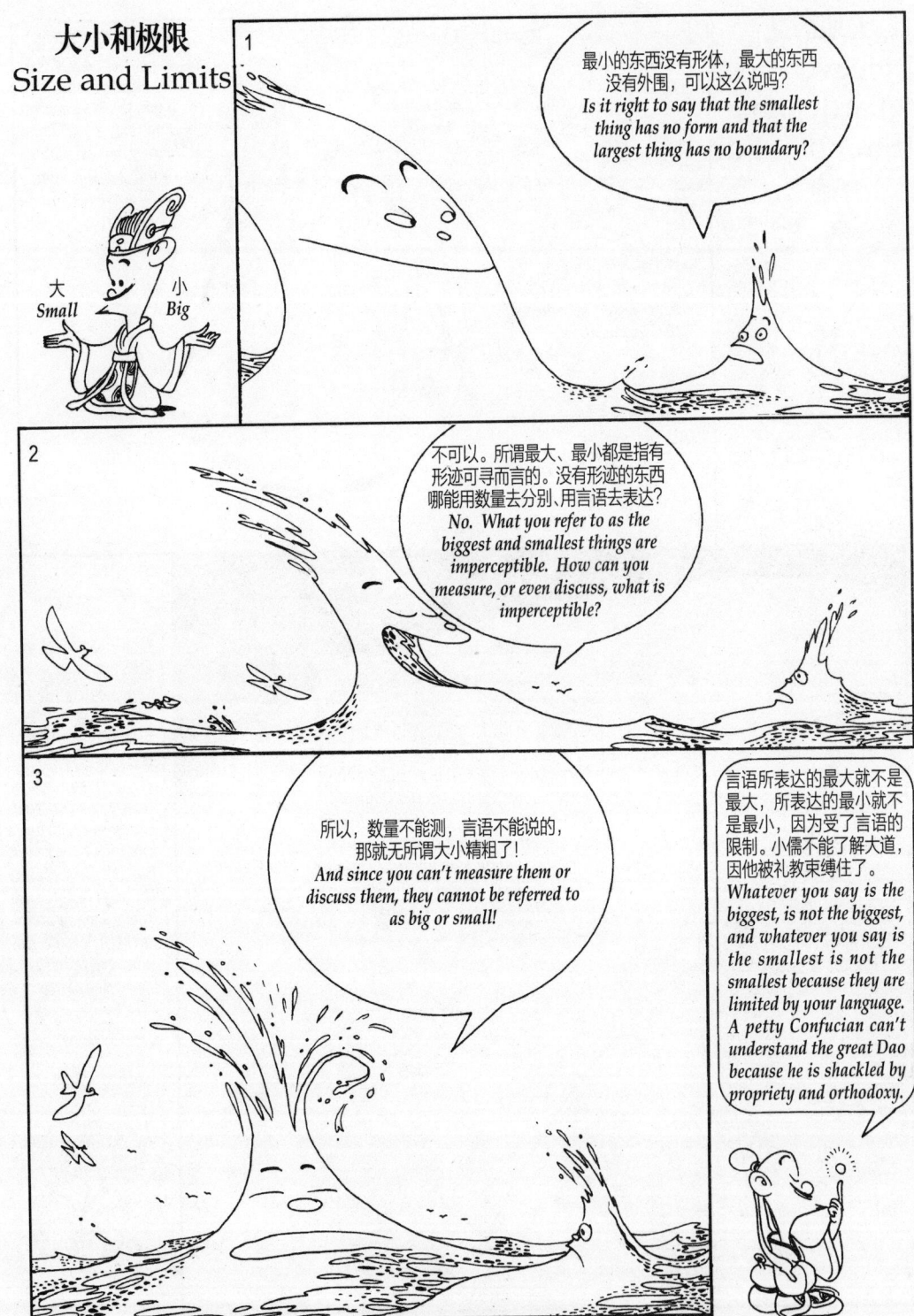

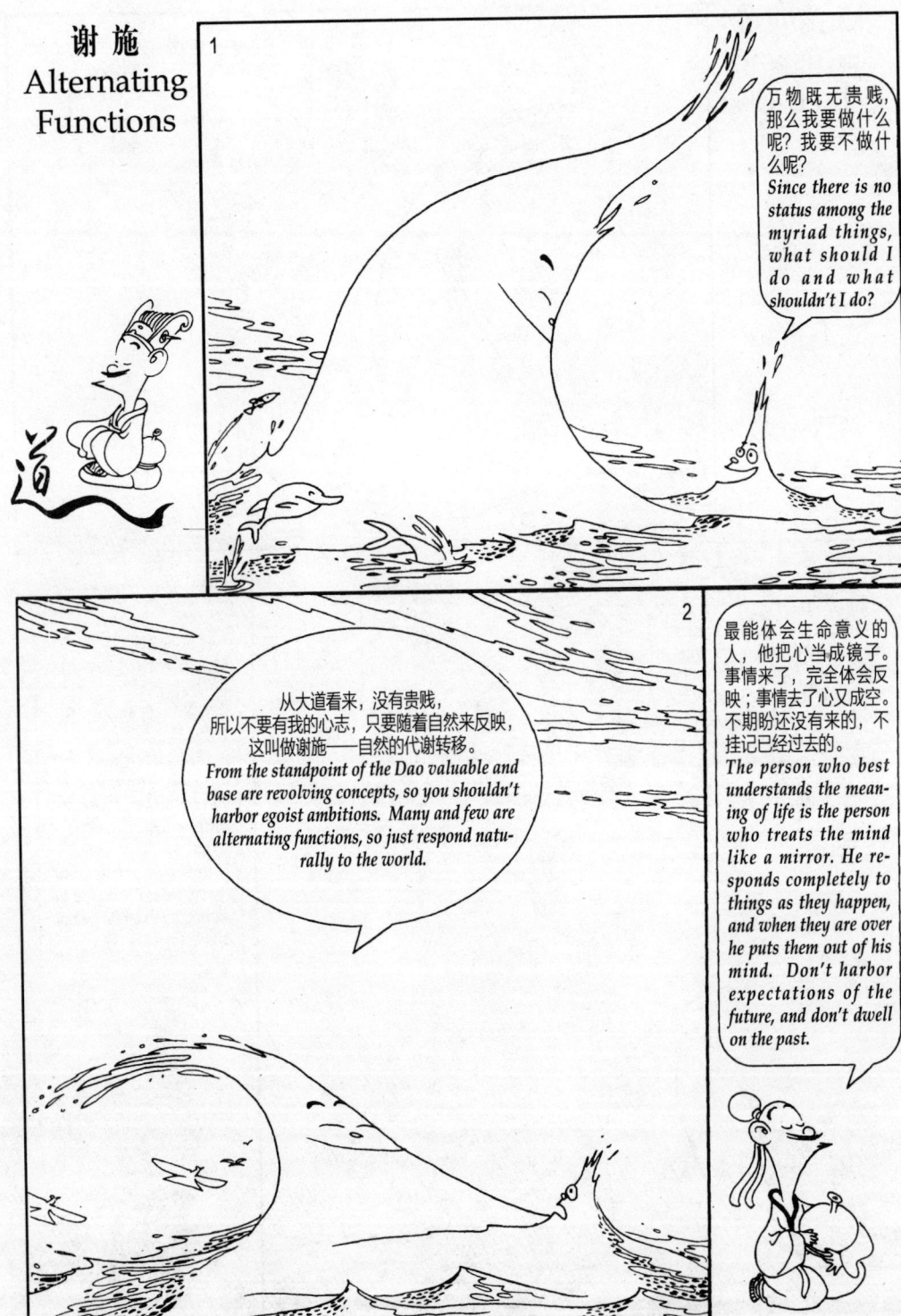

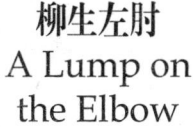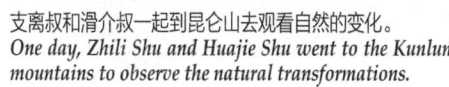

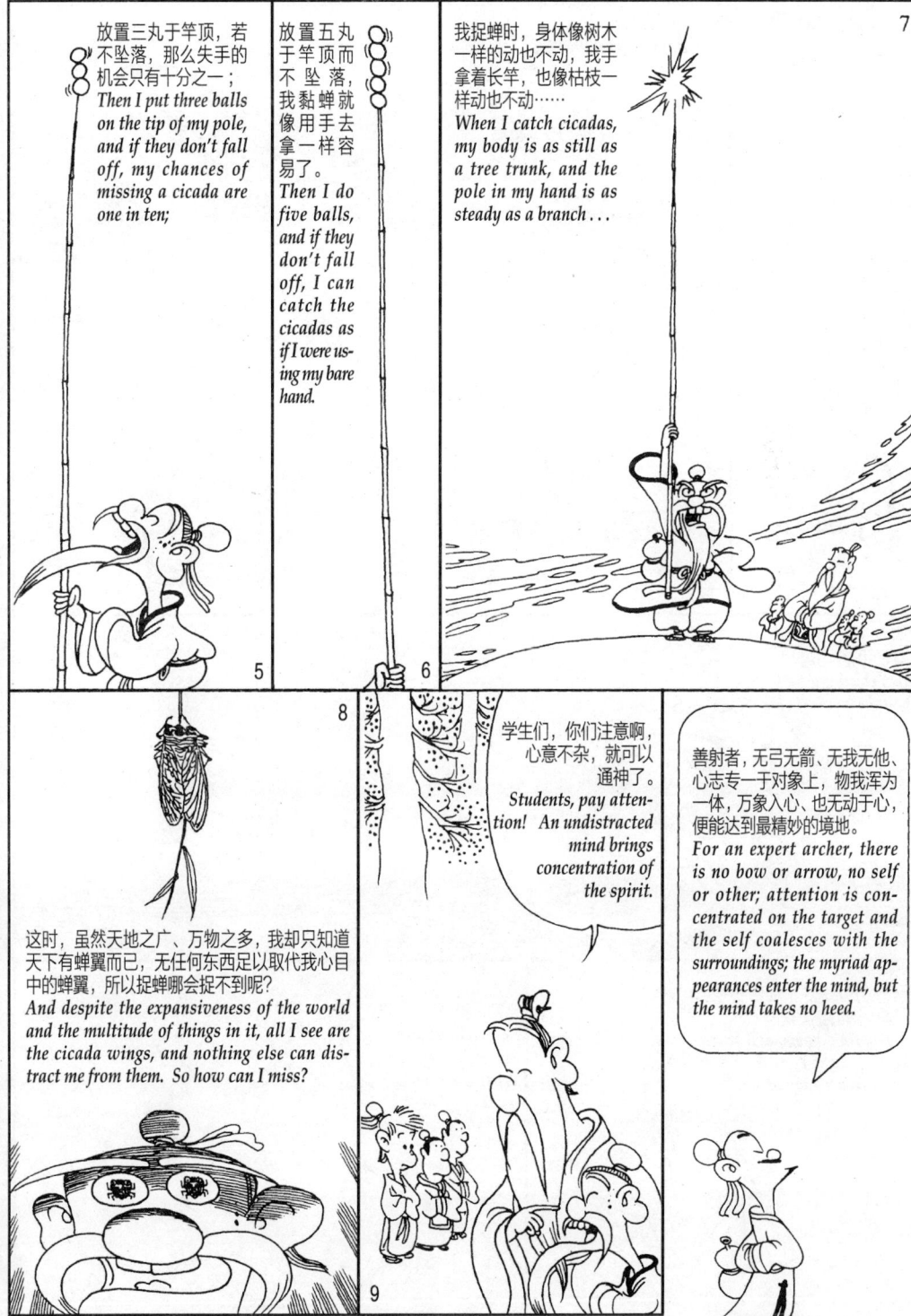

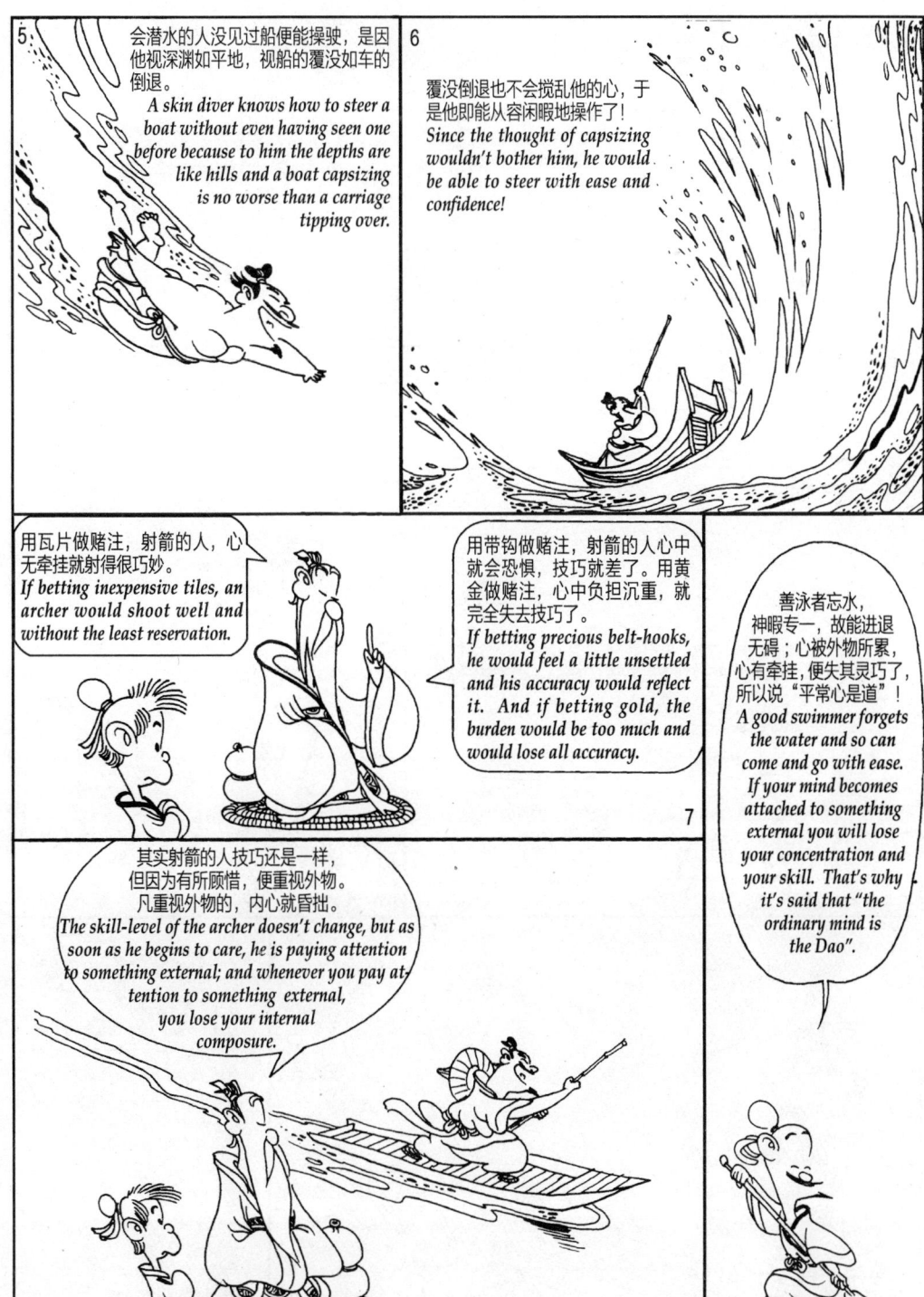

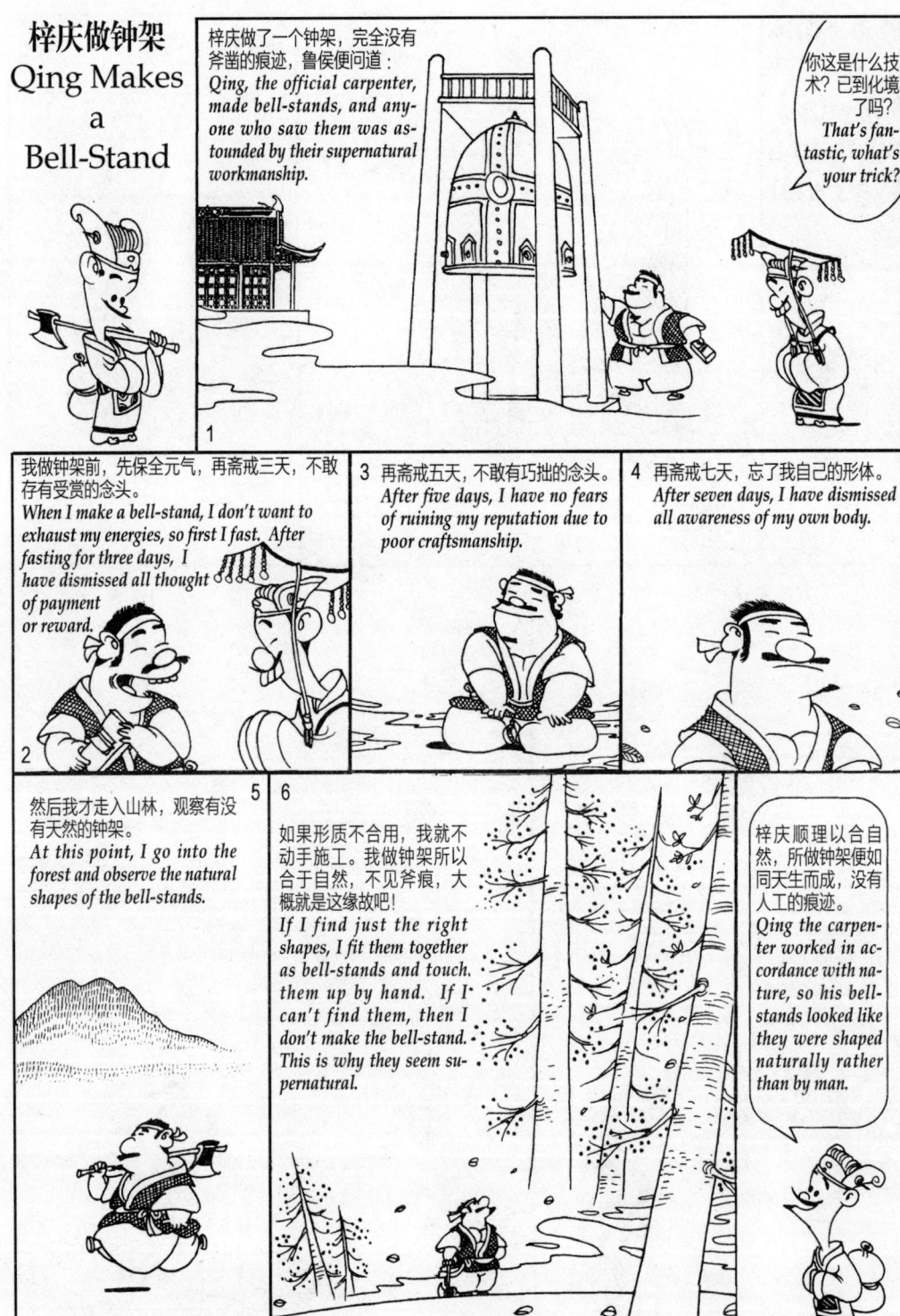

工倕的手指
Gong Chui's Fingers

工倕的手指和工具合而为一，不必用心去做，就能画出方圆。
Gong Chui's fingers became one with his tools, so without even trying, he created perfect shapes.

1

忘了脚的人，鞋子对他自然很舒适。
The shoes of a person who forgets his feet are naturally comfortable.

2

忘了腰的人，束带对他自然很舒适。
The belt of a person who forgets his waist is naturally comfortable.

3

忘了是非的人，他的心自然很舒适。
The mind of a person who forgets right and wrong is naturally comfortable.

4

5

忘了舒适的人，那是真舒适了。
The most comfortable of all is the person who forgets comfort altogether.

心不要强求专一，不要强求与外物契合，才是合乎自然之道。
Don't force your mind to concentrate, and don't force yourself to be in harmony with the external world. Just let it happen naturally.

百里奚养牛
Baili Xi Raises Oxen

百里奚不把"卑贱"放在心上,所以他养牛的时候,就把牛养得很肥。
When Baili Xi worked raising oxen, he didn't dwell on it being a lowly job, so they turned out big and plump.

秦穆公认为百里奚能够忘去卑贱,就把政事交给他,封他为"五羖大夫"。
Qin's Duke Mu was impressed by Baili Xi's being able to disregard his lowliness and so gave him a government position and a noble title.

百里奚做了五羖大夫以后,也没把"爵禄"放在心上,所以把政事办得很好。
As a nobleman, Baili Xi didn't dwell on his prestigious status, so his administration was very successful.

做事做官能忘却自己的卑贱、高贵,即能无我。爵禄不入于心,不求钱,不邀功,政事还会办不好吗?
If you can disregard your status, you will become selfless. If in doing government work, you don't dwell on status, seek wealth, or aim for great achievements, how can you fail?

知的极点
Breaking the Barriers

庄子说 自然的箫声

要学的人，是学他所不能学到的；
A student studies what he can't study;

躬行实践的人，是行他所不能行的；
A do-er does what he can't do;

辩论的人，是辩他所不能辩的。
A debater debates what he can't debate.

知的探求，要把目标定在他所不能知的境域，
A knowledge-seeker set his sights on what he can't know.

如果有不是这样的，他自然的本性就要遭受亏损。
If this weren't the case, natural equanimity would be lost.

自然的本性就是变化生生不息。重复着已经做过的、已经知道的，与死亡无异。
The nature of nature is constant change. If you do the same things or study the same things over and over, how are you different from a corpse?

至仁
Ultimate Benevolence

Ow!

对不起！
抱歉啊！
Ooops, I'm sorry!
Please excuse me!

踩了市人的脚，就得赔罪说对不起；
If you step on a stranger's foot, you must apologize and show remorse;

踩了哥哥的脚，就对他抚慰怜惜；
If you step on your older brother's foot, you must comfort him a bit;

老哥！把你的脚踩痛了吧？
Ooops, are you OK.?

哎呀！
Ow!

至礼没有人我之分，至义没有物我之分，至智不用谋略，至仁没有亲疏之别，至信不必以金玉为抵押品。
Ultimate propriety is to not distinguish between self and other; ultimate righteousness is to not distinguish between self and things; ultimate wisdom is to not scheme; ultimate benevolence is to not distinguish between remote and intimate; ultimate trust does not seek valuables as collateral.

踩了父母的脚就无须说对不起！
If you step on your father's foot, you don't have to do anything!

爱就是不必跟他说抱歉！
Love is not having to say you're sorry!

哎呀！
Ow!

不知的境域
The Realm of Ignorance

足所踩的只须鞋一般大的地，但还要依恃没踩到的地才能达到广远。
Your foot only needs a piece of ground the size of your shoe, but to go any distance, you also depend on the ground that the feet don't walk on.

1

人所知的很少，但还要依恃所不知的而后才能知道天道的自然。
We don't know much, and yet it is by relying on that which we don't know that we can come to understand nature.

2

知道大一，
知道大阴，
知道大目，
知道大均，
知道大方，
知道大信，
知道大定，
那就尽善尽美了。
Perfection is:
realizing the grand unity,
the grand mystery,
the grand vision,
the grand equanimity,
the grand magnanimity,
the grand trust, and
the grand serenity.

3

大一能贯通万物，大阴能解除万虑，大目能视无偏遗，大均能循顺万物本性，大方能为万物依附，大信能考而有实，大定能持守不挠。
To realize the grand unity is to understand the Dao, To realize the grand mystery is to unravel the mystery of the Dao, To realize the grand vision is to see the Dao, To realize the grand equanimity is to flow with the Dao, To realize the grand magnanimity is to experience the Dao, To realize the grand trust is find the truth in the Dao, To realize the grand serenity is to maintain the Dao.

4

人应顺乎天地，照彻万物，深藏道心，明己明彼。
We should all follow nature, be in accordance with the myriad things, conceal the Daoist mind, and understand ourselves and others.

5

在这种情境中自然的解悟好像未曾知解，无心的知好像无所知，无心的知才是真知。
In this kind of realm, resolving the mystery of the Dao is like the time before it was resolved, and realizing the Dao is like the time before it was realized—knowledge comes only after recognizing our ignorance.

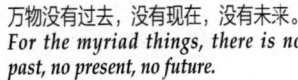

环中之道
The Cyclic Dao

1. 冉相氏悟出了环中之道，以应无穷之变。
The great sage Ran Xiang realized the significance of the cycle and how it is a sequential composition of unceasing transformations.

万物没有过去，没有现在，没有未来。
For the myriad things, there is no past, no present, no future.

2.

3. 形体与万物相合，真我不须臾离开。效法自然，而不有心效法自然。
没有自然的观念，也没有人的观念。
The body becomes one with the myriad things, and the genuine self doesn't leave even for a moment. Nature is emulated, but not intentionally. There isn't even an idea of nature or of people.

人返璞真性，顺物自成和外物契合，无始无终、无日无时。随物与时变化，内心宁静不变，即能不空不有。
The Dao is without beginning or end, without a motive force, and without time. To be in accord with it, we follow the myriad things on their cyclic path, forever changing and forever tranquil.

任公子钓大鱼
The Prince of Ren Goes Fishing

任公子做大钩和巨索，用五十条阉过的牛做饵，蹲在会稽山上投竿东海钓大鱼。
A prince of Ren once made a huge hook and a giant pole, used fifty steers as bait, crouched down on Kuaiji Mountain, tossed his line into the Eastern Sea, and fished for a big fish.

守了一年，终于有条大鱼上钩，鱼在海中卷起的波浪像山一样高。
After waiting patiently for a whole year, he got a bite, and it was an enormous fish that created waves as high as mountains.

呼啸！
whoosh!

任公子把鱼钩上，切成鱼片，从浙江以东到苍梧以北的人都吃饱了。
The prince drew up the fish, had it chopped into pieces, and it was enough to feed all the people for miles around.

喜欢传说的人，听了任公子的故事，无不奔走相告。
People who like legends, love the prince of Ren story and always run off to tell others about it.

那条鱼真的好大好大！
I'm telling you, that fish was huge!

至于那些经常拿着小鱼竿钓小鱼的人，他就根本不相信。
As for those who fish for small fish with small poles, they don't believe any of it.

胡说八道！
Nonsense!

小儒不能通大道，因为他只凭一己有限的知识经验，去否定超越知识的大道。
Petty scholastics will never understand the great Dao! They go on their tiny bit of limited knowledge and experience, and deny the great Dao that is beyond knowledge.

孔子的变化
Confucius Changes

孔子行年六十岁而有六十岁的变化。
Confucius lived for sixty years, and he changed for sixty years.

从前认为对的，现在不敢说对的了；现在认为对的，也不敢说是从前的不对。
What he had thought was wrong in the past he might have thought to be right in the present. What he thought to be right in the present, he might have thought was wrong in the past.

孔子到现在还是使用知识、劳苦心智吗？
Did Confucius work hard to fulfill his ambitions and put his knowledge to use. Confucius was beyond that.

孔子早就超越这境界了。
Confucius was beyond that.

惠子问庄子说：
Huizi asked Zhuangzi:

他认为明辨是非，不过是服人之口而已，不能服人之心。如要使人心服，必须合乎自然的大道才行。
He felt that although debating right and wrong could win verbal assent, it couldn't win people's hearts. If you want to win people's hearts, you must act in accordance with the natural Dao.

使用心智、劳苦心智，是一种较低的层次。智者应该超越这个层次。
Putting intelligence to use is a lesser stratum. A wise person goes beyond this stratum.

生活为贵
名位为轻
Life Is Most Important

尧把天下让给许由，但许由不接受……
Yao wished to abdicate and hand the world over the Xu You, but Xu You wouldn't accept . . .

于是尧又想把天下让给子州支父……
So Yao tried Zizhou Zhifu ...

让我做天子，还可以。
I would accept ...

不过，我正患有深忧之病，将要医治，没有时间来治理天下。
But I have a very worrisome illness. Because I've got to get that cured, I'm afraid I won't have time to govern the land.

天下最大的权力名位莫大于天子之位了，而不肯以它来交换生命，这是有道的人所以和凡俗不同的地方。
Emperor is the most powerful position in the world, but there are some who would refuse to exchange their lives for it. This is what separates a person of the Dao from a common person.

逐利之夫
The Man Who Pursued Profit

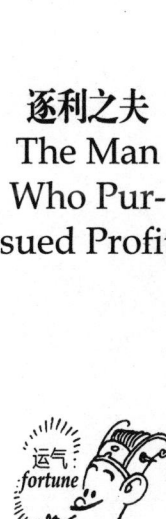

运气
fortune

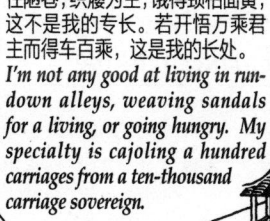

宋人曹商出使秦国，秦王喜欢他，赐他车辆百乘。
Cao Shang of Song was sent as emissary to Qin. The Qin king liked him very much and so bestowed him with one hundred carriages.

住陋巷，织屦为生，饿得颈枯面黄，这不是我的专长。若开悟万乘君主而得车百乘，这是我的长处。
I'm not any good at living in rundown alleys, weaving sandals for a living, or going hungry. My specialty is cajoling a hundred carriages from a ten-thousand carriage sovereign.

秦王有病召医，能够使他的毒疮溃散的，可获得车辆一乘……
When the king gets an illness that needs cured, he gives a carriage away to the person who can cure him...

舐好痔疮的可获得车辆五乘，所医治的愈卑下，所得的车辆愈多。
To the person who licks his boils, he gives five carriages. The more demeaning the task, the greater the number of carriages.

你难道是医治秦王的痔疮？为什么得到这么多车辆？
What despicable thing did you do to get so many carriages?

为求名利外物，人往往会违背自己的本性去做卑下低贱的事。君子恬淡志远，有所为，也有所不为！
People often go against their own nature and do demeaning and despicable things in pursuit of profit and status. A gentleman is easygoing and highminded. There are things he will do, and there are things he won't do.

附录·延伸阅读
APPENDIX Further reading

此部分为本书图画页的延伸阅读，各段首所示的页码与图画页对应。

P1　庄子者，蒙人也，名周。周尝为蒙漆园吏，与梁惠王、齐宣王同时。其学无所不窥，然其要本归于老子之言。故其著书十余万言，大抵率寓言也。作渔父、盗跖、胠箧，以诋訿孔子之徒，以明老子之术。畏累虚、亢桑子之属，皆空语无事实，然善属书离辞，指事情类，用剽剥儒墨，虽当以适己，故自王公大人不能器之。

《汉·司马迁◎史记》

P3　夫庄子者，可谓知本矣，故未始藏其狂言，言虽无会而独应者也。夫应而非会，则虽当无用；言非物事，则虽高不行；与я寂然不动，不得已而后起者，固有间矣，斯可谓知无心者也。夫心无为，则随感而应，应随其时，言唯谨尔。故与化为体，流万代而冥物，岂曾设对独遘而游谈乎方外哉！此其所以不经而为百家之冠也。

《晋·郭象◎庄子序》

P4　庄子者，姓庄，名周，（太史公云：字子休。）梁国蒙县人也。六国时，为漆园吏，与魏惠王、齐宣王、楚威王同时，（李颐云：与齐愍王同时。）齐楚尝聘以为相，不应。时人皆尚游说，庄子独高尚其事，优游自得，依老氏之旨，著书十余万言，以逍遥自然无为齐物而已；大抵皆寓言，归之于理，不可案文责也。

《唐·陆德明◎庄子序》

P5　夫庄子者，所以申道德之深根，述重玄之妙旨，畅无为之恬淡，明独化之窅冥，钳揵九流，括囊百氏，谅区中之至教，实象外之微言者也。

其人姓庄，名周，字子休，生宋国睢阳蒙县，师长桑公子，受号南华仙人。当战国之初，降周之末，叹苍生之业薄，伤道德之陵夷，乃慷慨发愤，爰著斯论。其言大而博，其旨深而远，非下士之所闻，岂浅识之能究！

《唐·成玄英◎庄子序》

P6　小知不及大知，小年不及大年。奚以知其然也？朝菌不知晦朔，蟪蛄不知春秋，此小年也。楚之南有冥灵者，以五百岁为春，五百岁为秋；上古有大椿者，以八千岁为春，八千岁为秋。而彭祖乃今以久特闻，众人匹之，不亦悲乎！

《庄子◎逍遥游第一》

P8 汤之问棘也是已。穷发之北有冥海者，天池也。有鱼焉，其广数千里，未有知其修者，其名为鲲。

有鸟焉，其名为鹏，背若太山，翼若垂天之云，搏扶摇羊角而上者九万里，绝云气，负青天，然后图南，且适南冥也。斥鴳笑之曰："彼且奚适也？我腾跃而上，不过数仞而下，翱翔蓬蒿之间，此亦飞之至也。而彼且奚适也？"此小大之辩也。

《庄子◎逍遥游第一》

P9-P10 惠子谓庄子曰："魏王贻我大瓠之种，我树之成而实五石，以盛水浆，其坚不能自举也；剖之以为瓢，则瓠落无所容。非不呺然大也，吾为其无用而掊之。"

庄子曰："夫子固拙于用大矣。宋人有善为不龟手之药者，世世以洴澼絖为事。客闻之，请买其方百金。聚族而谋曰：'我世世为洴澼絖，不过数金；今一朝而鬻技百金，请与之。'客得之，以说吴王。越有难，吴王使之将，冬与越人水战，大败越人，裂地而封之。能不龟手，一也；或以封，或不免于洴澼絖，则所用之异也。今子有五石之瓠，何不虑以为大樽而浮乎江湖，而忧其瓠落无所容？则夫子犹有蓬之心也夫！"

《庄子◎逍遥游第一》

P11-P12 宋人有善为不龟手之药者，世世以洴澼絖为事。客闻之，请买其方百金。聚族而谋曰："我世世为洴澼絖，不过数金；今一朝而鬻技百金，请与之。"客得之，以说吴王。越有难，吴王使之将，冬与越人水战，大败越人，裂地而封之。能不龟手，一也；或以封，或不免于洴澼絖，则所用之异也。

《庄子◎逍遥游第一》

P13-P14 惠子谓庄子曰："吾有大树，人谓之樗。其大本拥肿而不中绳墨，其小枝卷曲而不中规矩，立之涂，匠者不顾。今子之言，大而无用，众所同去也。"

庄子曰："子独不见狸狌乎？卑身而伏，以候敖者；东西跳梁，不辟高下；中于机辟，死于罔罟。今夫斄牛，其大若垂天之云。此能为大矣，而不能执鼠。今子有大树，患其无用，何不树之于无何有之乡，广莫之野，彷徨乎无为其侧，逍遥乎寝卧其下。不夭斤斧，物无害者，无所可用，安所困苦哉！"

《庄子◎逍遥游第一》

P16 宋人资章甫而适诸越，越人断发文身，无所用之。尧治天下之民，平海内之政，往见四子藐姑射之山，汾水之阳，窅然丧其天下焉。

《庄子◎逍遥游第一》

P17-P19 南郭子綦隐机而坐，仰天而嘘，荅焉似丧其耦。颜成子游立侍乎前，曰："何居乎？形固可使如槁木，而心固可使如死灰乎？今之隐机者，非昔之隐机者也。"

子綦曰："偃，不亦善乎，而问之也，今者吾丧我，汝知之乎？女闻人籁而未闻地籁，女闻地籁而未闻天籁夫！"

子游曰："敢问其方。"

子綦曰："夫大块噫气，其名为风，是唯无作，作则万窍怒号。而独不闻之翏翏乎？山林之畏佳，大木百围之窍穴，似鼻，似口，似耳，似枅，似圈，似臼，似洼者，似污者；激者，謞者，叱者，吸者，叫者，譹者，宎者，咬者，前者唱于而随者唱喁。泠风则小和，飘风则大和，厉风济则众窍为虚。而独不见之调调，之刁刁乎？"

《庄子◎齐物论第二》

P20 古之人，其知有所至矣。恶乎至？有以为未始有物者，至矣，尽矣，不可以加矣。其次以为有物矣，而未始有封也。其次以为有封焉，而未始有是非也。是非之彰也，道之所以亏也。道之所以亏，爱之所以成。果且有成与亏乎哉？果且无成与亏乎哉？有成与亏，故昭氏之鼓琴也；无成与亏，故昭氏之不鼓琴也。

《庄子◎齐物论第二》

P21-P22 啮缺问乎王倪曰："子知物之所同是乎？"
曰："吾恶乎知之！"
"子知子之所不知邪？"
曰："吾恶乎知之！"
"然则物无知邪？"
曰："吾恶乎知之！"
虽然，尝试言之。庸讵知吾所谓知之非不知邪？庸讵知吾所谓不知之非知邪？
且吾尝试问乎女：民湿寝则腰疾偏死，鳅然乎哉？木处则惴栗恂惧，猿猴然乎哉？三者孰知正处？民食刍豢，麋鹿食荐，蝍蛆甘带，鸱鸦嗜鼠，四者孰知正味？猿猵狙以为雌，麋与鹿交，鳅与鱼游。毛嫱丽姬，人之所美也；鱼见之深入，鸟见之高飞，麋鹿见之决骤。四者孰知天下之正色哉？自我观之，仁义之端，是非之涂，樊然殽乱，吾恶能知其辩！

《庄子◎齐物论第二》

P23 且吾尝试问乎女：民湿寝则腰疾偏死，鳅然乎哉？木处则惴栗恂惧，猿猴然乎哉？三者孰知正处？民食刍豢，麋鹿食荐，蝍蛆甘带，鸱鸦嗜鼠，四者孰知正味？猿猵狙以为雌，麋与鹿交，鳅与鱼游。毛嫱丽姬，人之所美也；鱼见之深入，鸟见之高飞，麋鹿见之决骤。四者孰知天下之正色哉？自我观之，仁义之端，是非之涂，樊然殽乱，吾恶能知其辩！

《庄子◎齐物论第二》

P24 予尝为女妄言之，女以妄听之。奚旁日月，挟宇宙？为其吻合，置其滑涽，以隶相尊。众人役役，圣人愚芚，参万岁而一成纯。万物尽然，而以是相蕴。
予恶乎知说生之非惑邪！予恶乎知恶死之非弱丧而不知归者邪！丽之姬，艾封人之子也。晋国之始得之也，涕泣沾襟；及其至于王所，与王同筐床，食刍豢，而后悔其泣也。予恶乎知夫死者不悔其始之蕲生乎！

《庄子◎齐物论第二》

P25 梦饮酒者，旦而哭泣；梦哭泣者，旦而田猎。方其梦也，不知其梦也。梦之中又占其梦焉，觉而后知其梦也。且有大觉而后知此其大梦也，而愚者自以为觉，窃窃然知之。君乎，牧乎，固哉！丘也与女，皆梦也；予谓女梦，亦梦也。是其言也，其名为吊诡。万世之后而一遇大圣，知其解者，是旦暮遇之也。

《庄子◎齐物论第二》

P26 罔两问景曰:"曩子行,今子止;曩子坐,今子起;何其无特操与?"景曰:"吾有待而然者邪?吾所待又有待而然者邪?吾待蛇蚹蜩翼邪?恶识所以然!恶识所以不然!"

《庄子◎齐物论第二》

P27 昔者庄周梦为胡蝶,栩栩然胡蝶也,自喻适志与!不知周也。俄然觉,则蘧蘧然周也。不知周之梦为胡蝶,胡蝶之梦为周与?周与胡蝶,则必有分矣。此之谓物化。

《庄子◎齐物论第二》

P28 唯达者知通唯一,为是不用而寓诸庸。庸也者,用也;用也者,通也;通也者,得也;适得而几矣。因是已。已而不知其然,谓之道。劳神明为一而不知其同也,谓之朝三。何谓朝三?
狙公赋芧,曰:"朝三而暮四,"众狙皆怒。曰:"然则朝四而暮三,"众狙皆悦。名实未亏而喜怒为用,亦因是也。是以圣人和之以是非而休乎天钧,是之谓两行。

《庄子◎齐物论第二》

P29-P31 昭文之鼓琴也,师旷之枝策也,惠子之据梧也,三子之知几乎,皆其盛者也,故载之末年。
庖丁为文惠君解牛,手之所触,肩之所倚,足之所履,膝之所踦,砉然向然,奏刀騞然,莫不中音。合于桑林之舞,乃中经首之会。
文惠君曰:"嘻,善哉!技盖至此乎?"
庖丁释刀对曰:"臣之所好者道也,进乎技矣。始臣之解牛之时,所见无非全牛者。三年之后,未尝见全牛也。方今之时,臣以神遇而不以目视,官知止而神欲行。依乎天理,批大郤,导大窾,因其固然。技经肯綮之未尝,而况大軱乎!良庖岁更刀,割也;族庖月更刀,折也。今臣之刀十九年矣,所解数千牛矣,而刀刃若新发于硎。彼节者有闲,而刀刃者无厚;以无厚入有闲,恢恢乎其于游刃必有余地矣,是以十九年而刀刃若新发于硎。虽然,每至于族,吾见其难为,怵然为戒,视为止,行为迟。动刀甚微,謋然已解,如土委地。提刀而立,为之四顾,为之踌躇满志,善刀而藏之。"
文惠君曰:"善哉!吾闻庖丁之言,得养生焉。"

《庄子◎养生主第三》

P32 指穷于为薪,火传也,不知其尽也。

《庄子◎养生主第三》

P33 泽雉十步一啄,百步一饮,不蕲畜乎樊中。神虽王,不善也。

《庄子◎养生主第三》

P34-P35 颜阖将傅卫灵公大子,而问于蘧伯玉曰:"有人于此,其德天杀。与之为无方,则危吾国;与之为有方,则危吾身。其知适足以知人之过,而不知其所以过。若然者,吾奈之何?"
蘧伯玉曰:"善哉问乎!戒之,慎之,正女身也哉!形莫若就,心莫若和。虽然,之二者有患。就不欲入,和不欲出。形就而入,且为颠为灭,为崩为蹶。心和而出,且为声为名,为妖为孽。彼且为婴儿,亦与之为婴儿;彼且为无町畦,亦与之为无町畦;彼且为无崖,亦与之为无崖。达之,入于无疵。汝不知夫螳螂乎?怒其臂以当车辙,不知其不胜任也,是其才之美者也。戒之,慎之,积伐而美者以犯之，几矣。"

《庄子◎人间世第四》

P36 夫爱马者，以筐盛矢，以蜄盛溺。适有蚊虻仆缘，而拊之不时，则缺衔毁首碎胸。意有所至而爱有所亡，可不慎邪！

《庄子◎人间世第四》

P37-P38 匠石之齐，至于曲辕，见栎社树。其大蔽数千牛，絜之百围，其高临山十仞而后有枝，其可以为舟者旁十数。观者如市，匠伯不顾，遂行不辍。

弟子厌观之，走及匠石，曰："自吾执斧斤以随夫子，未尝见材如此其美也。先生不肯视，行不辍，何邪？"

曰："已矣，勿言之矣！散木也，以为舟则沉，以为棺椁则速腐，以为器则速毁，以为门户则液樠，以为柱则蠹。是不材之木也，无所可用，故能若是之寿。"

匠石归，栎社见梦曰："女将恶乎比予哉？若将比予于文木邪？夫柤梨橘柚，果蓏之属，实熟则剥，剥则辱；大枝折，小枝泄。此以其能苦其生者也，故不终其天年而中道夭，自掊击于世俗者也。物莫不若是。且予求无所可用久矣，几死，乃今得之，为予大用。使予也而有用，且得有此大也邪？且也若与予也皆物也，奈何哉其相物也？而几死之散人，又恶知散木！"

《庄子◎人间世第四》

P39-P40 宋有荆氏者，宜楸柏桑。其拱把而上者，求狙猴之杙者斩之；三围四围，求高名之丽者斩之；七围八围，贵人富商之家求樿傍者斩之。故未终其天年，而中道之夭于斧斤，此材之患也。

故解之牛之白颡者与豚之亢鼻者，与人有痔病者不可以适河。此皆巫祝以知之矣，所以为不祥也。此乃神人之所以为大祥也。

《庄子◎人间世第四》

P41 支离疏者，颐隐于脐，肩高于顶，会撮指天，五管在上，两髀为胁。挫针治繲，足以糊口；鼓筴播精，足以食十人。上征武士，则支离疏攘臂而游其间；上有大役，则支离以有常疾不受功；上与病者粟，则受三钟与十束薪。夫支离其形者，犹足以养其身，终其天年，又况支离其德者乎！

《庄子◎人间世第四》

P42 山木自寇也，膏火自煎也。桂可食，故伐之；漆可用，故割之。人皆知有用之用，而莫知无用之用也。

《庄子◎人间世第四》

P43 汝不知夫养虎者乎？不敢以生物与之，为其杀之之怒也；不敢以全物与之，为其决之之怒也；时其饥饱，达其怒心。虎之与人异类而媚养己者，顺也；故其杀者，逆也。

《庄子◎人间世第四》

P44 鲁有兀者叔山无趾，踵见仲尼。仲尼曰："子不谨，前既犯患若是矣。虽今来，何及矣！"

无趾曰："吾唯不知务而轻用吾身，吾是以亡足。今吾来也，犹有尊足者存，吾是以务全之也。夫天无不覆，地无不载，吾以夫子为天地，安知夫子之犹若是也！"

孔子曰："丘则陋矣。夫子胡不入乎，请讲以所闻！"

无趾出。孔子曰："弟子勉之！夫无趾，兀者也，犹务学以复补前行之恶，而况全德之人乎！"

《庄子◎德充符第五》

P45 泉涸，鱼相与处于陆，相呴以湿，相濡以沫，不如相忘于江湖，与其誉尧而非桀也，不如两忘而化其道。

《庄子◎大宗师第六》

P46 子贡曰："然则夫子何方之依？"

孔子曰："丘，天之戮民也。虽然，吾与汝共之。"

子贡曰："敢问其方。"

孔子曰："鱼相造乎水，人相造乎道。相造乎水者，穿池而养给；相造乎道者，无事而生定。故曰，鱼相忘乎江湖，人相忘乎道术。"

《庄子◎大宗师第六》

P47 子舆与子桑友，而霖雨十日。子舆曰："子桑殆病矣！"裹饭而往食之。至子桑之门，则若歌若哭，鼓琴曰："父邪！母邪！天乎！人乎！"有不任其声而趋举其诗焉。

子舆入，曰："子之歌诗，何故若是？"

曰："吾思夫使我至此极者而弗得也。父母岂欲吾贫哉？天无私覆，地无私载，天地岂私贫我哉？求其为之者而不得也。然而至此极者，命也夫！"

《庄子◎大宗师第六》

P48 肩吾见狂接舆，狂接舆曰："日中始何以语女？"

肩吾曰："告我君人者以己出经式义度，人孰敢不听而化诸！"

狂接舆曰："是欺德也；其于治天下也，犹涉海凿河而使蚊负山也。夫圣人之治也，治外乎？正而后行，确乎能其事者而已矣。且鸟高飞以避矰弋之害，鼷鼠深穴乎神丘之下以避熏凿之患，而曾二虫之无知！"

《庄子◎应帝王第七》

P49 骈于辩者，累瓦结绳窜句，游心于坚白同异之闲，而敝跬誉无用之言非乎？而杨墨是已。故此皆多骈旁枝之道，非天下之至正也。

彼正正者，不失其性命之情。故合者不为骈，而枝者不为跂；长者不为有余，短者不为不足。是故凫胫虽短，续之则忧；鹤胫虽长，断之则悲。故性长非所断，性短非所续，无所去忧也。意仁义其非人情乎！彼仁人何其多忧也？

《庄子◎骈拇第八》

P50 自三代以下者，天下莫不以物易其性矣，小人则以身殉利，士则以身殉名，大夫则以身殉家，圣人则以身殉天下。故此数子者，事业不同，名声异号，其于伤性以身为殉，一也。臧与穀，二人相与牧羊而俱亡其羊。问臧奚事，则挟策读书；问穀奚事，则博塞以游。二人者，事业不同，其于亡羊均也。

《庄子◎骈拇第八》

P51-P52 故跖之徒问于跖曰:"盗亦有道乎?"跖曰:"何适而无有道邪!"夫妄意室中之藏,圣也;入先,勇也;出后,义也;知可否,知也;分均,仁也。五者不备而能成大盗者,天下未之有也。由是观之,善人不得圣人之道不立,跖不得圣人之道不行;天下之善人少而不善人多,则圣人之利天下也少而害天下也多。

《庄子◎胠箧第十》

P53 故曰,唇竭则齿寒,鲁酒薄而邯郸围,圣人生而大盗起。掊击圣人,纵舍盗贼,而天下始治矣。夫川竭而谷虚,丘夷而渊实。圣人已死,则大盗不起,天下平而无故矣。

许慎注淮南云:楚会诸侯,鲁赵俱献酒于楚王。鲁酒薄而赵酒厚,楚之主酒过求酒于赵,赵不与。吏怒,乃以赵厚酒易鲁薄酒,奏之。楚王以赵酒薄,故围邯郸也。

《庄子◎胠箧第十》

P54 (上略)
黄帝退,捐天下,筑特室,席白茅,闲居三月,复往邀之。

广成子南首而卧,黄帝顺下风膝行而进,再拜稽首而问曰:"闻君子达于至道,敢问,治身奈何而可以长久?"广成子蹶然而起,曰:"善哉问乎!来!吾语女至道。至道之精,窈窈冥冥;至道之极,昏昏默默。无视无听,抱神以静,形将自正。必静必清,无劳女形,无摇女精,乃可以长生。"

《庄子◎在宥第十一》

P55 夫有土者,有大物也。有大物者,不可以物;物而不物,故能物物。明乎物物者之非物也,岂独治天下百姓而已哉!出入六合,游乎九州,独往独来,是谓独有。独有之人,是谓至贵。

大人之教,若形之于影,声之于响。有问而应之,尽其所怀,为天下配。处乎无响,行乎无方。挈汝适复之挠挠,以游无端;出入无旁,与日无始;颂论形躯,合乎大同,大同而无己。无己,恶乎得有有!睹有者,昔之君子;睹无者,天地之友。

《庄子◎在宥第十一》

P56-P57 桓公读书于堂上。轮扁斲轮于堂下,释椎凿而上,问桓公曰:"敢问,公之所读者何言邪?"

公曰:"圣人之言也。"
曰:"圣人在乎?"
公曰:"已死矣。"
曰:"然则君子所读者,古人之糟魄已夫!"
桓公曰:"寡人读书,轮人安得议乎!有说则可,无说则死。"
轮扁曰:"臣也以臣之事观之。斲轮,徐则甘而不固,疾则苦而不入。不徐不疾,得之于手而应于心,口不能言,有数存焉于其间。臣不能以喻臣之子,臣之子亦不能受之于臣,是以行年七十而老斲轮。古之人与其不可传也死矣,然则君之所读者,古人之糟魄已夫!"

《庄子◎天道第十三》

P58 天其运乎?地其处乎?日月其争于所乎?孰主张是?孰维纲是?孰居无事推而行事?意者其

有机缄而不得已邪？意者其运转而不能自止邪？云者为雨乎？雨者为云乎？孰隆施是？孰居无事淫乐而劝是？风起北方，一西一东，有上彷徨，孰嘘吸是？孰居无事而披拂是？敢问何故？

《庄子◎天运第十四》

P59 孔子见老聃而语仁义。老聃曰："夫播穅眯目，则天地四方易位矣；蚊虻噆肤，则通昔不寐矣。夫仁义惨然乃愤吾心，乱莫大焉。吾子使天下无失其朴，吾子亦放风而动，总德而立矣，又奚傑然若负建鼓而求亡子者邪？夫鹄不日浴而白，乌不日黔而黑。黑白之朴，不足以为辩；名誉之观，不足以为广。"

《庄子◎天运第十四》

P60 孔子见老聃归，三日不谈。弟子问曰："夫子见老聃，亦将何规哉？"

孔子曰："吾乃今于是乎见龙！龙，合而成体，散而成章，乘云气而养乎阴阳予口张而不能嗋，予又何规老聃哉！"

《庄子◎天运第十四》

P61 河伯曰："何谓天？何谓人？"

北海若曰："牛马四足，是谓天；落马首，穿牛鼻，是谓人。

故曰，无以人灭天，无以故灭命，无以得殉名。谨守而勿矣，是谓反其真。"

《庄子◎秋水第十七》

P62-P63 夔谓蚿曰："吾以一足趻踔而行，予无如矣。今子之使万足，独奈何？"

蚿曰："不然。子不见夫唾者乎？喷则大者如珠，小者如雾，杂而下者不可胜数也。今予动吾天机，而不知其所以然。"

蚿谓蛇曰："吾以众足行，而不及子之无足，何也？"

蛇曰："夫天机之所动，何可易邪，吾安用足哉！"

蛇谓风曰："予动吾脊胁而行，则有似也。今子蓬蓬然起于北海，蓬蓬然入于南海，而似无有，何也？"

风曰："然。予蓬蓬然起于北海而入于南海也，然而指我则胜我，鳅我亦胜我。虽然，夫折大木，蜚大屋者，唯我能也，故以众小不胜为大胜也。为大胜者，唯圣人能之。"

《庄子◎秋水第十七》

P64-P65 孔子游于匡，宋人围之数匝，而弦歌不惙。子路入见，曰："何夫子之娱也？"

孔子曰："来！吾语女。我讳穷久矣，而不免，命也；求通久矣，而不得，时也。当尧舜而天下无穷人，非知得也；当桀纣而天下无通人，非知失也；时势适然。夫水行不避蛟龙者，渔父之勇也；陆行不避兕虎者，猎夫之勇也；白刃交于前，视死若生者，烈士之勇也；知穷之有命，知通之有时，临大难而不惧者，圣人之勇也。由处矣，吾命有所制矣。"

无几何，将甲者进，辞曰："以为阳虎也，故围之。今非也，请辞而退。"

《庄子◎秋水第十七》

P66-P68 公孙龙问于魏牟曰："龙少学先生之道，长而明仁义之行；合同异，离坚白；然不然，可不可；困百家之知，穷众口之辩；吾自以为至达已。今吾闻庄子之言，汒焉异之。不知论之不及与，知之弗若与？今吾无所开吾喙，敢问其方。"

公子牟隐机太息，仰天而笑曰："子独不闻夫坎井之蛙乎？谓东海之鳖曰：'吾乐与！出跳梁乎井干之上，入休乎缺甃之崖；赴水则接腋持颐，蹶泥则没足灭跗；还虷蟹与科斗，莫吾能若也。且夫擅一壑之水，而跨跱坎井之乐，此亦至矣，夫子奚不时来入观乎！'东海之鳖左足未入，而右膝已絷矣。于是逡巡而却，告之海曰：'夫千里之远，不足以举其大；千仞之高，不足以极其深。禹之时十年九潦，而水弗为加益；汤之时八年七旱，而崖不为加损。夫不为顷久推移，不以多少进退者，此亦东海之大乐也。'于是坎井之蛙闻之，适适然惊，规规然自失也。

且夫知不知是非之竟，而犹欲观于庄子之言，是犹使蚊虻负山，商蚷驰河也，必不胜任矣。且夫知不知论极妙之言而自适一时之利者，是非坎井之蛙与？且彼方跐黄泉而登大皇，无南无北，奭然四解，沦于不测；无东无西，始于玄冥，反于大通。子乃规规然求之以察，索之以辩，是直用管窥天，用锥指地也，不亦小乎！子往矣！

《庄子◎秋水第十七》

P69 且子独不闻夫寿陵余子之学行于邯郸与？未得国能，又失其故行矣，直匍匐而归耳。

《庄子◎秋水第十七》

P70-P71 惠子相梁，庄子往见之。或谓惠子曰："庄子来，欲代子相。"于是惠子恐，搜于国中三日三夜。

庄子往见之，曰："南方有鸟，其名为鹓鶵，子知之乎？夫鹓鶵，发于南海而飞于北海，非梧桐不止，非练实不食，非醴泉不饮。于是鸱得腐鼠，鹓鶵过之，仰而视之曰：'吓！'今子欲以子之梁国而吓我邪？"

《庄子◎秋水第十七》

P72 庄子与惠子游于濠梁之上。庄子曰："鲦鱼出游从容，是鱼之乐也。"

惠子曰："子非鱼，安知鱼之乐？"

庄子曰："子非我，安知我不知鱼之乐？"

惠子曰："我非子，固不知子矣；子固非鱼也，子之不知鱼之乐，全矣。"

庄子曰："请循其本。子曰'汝安知鱼乐'云者，既已知吾知之而问我，我知之濠上也。"

《庄子◎秋水第十七》

P73-P74 庄子之楚，见空髑髅，髐然有形，撽以马捶，因而问之，曰："夫子贪生失理，而为此乎？将子有亡国之事，斧钺之诛，而为此乎？将子有不善之行，愧遗父母妻子之丑，而为此乎？将子有冻馁之患，而为此乎？将子之春秋故及此乎？"

于是语卒，援髑髅，枕而卧。夜半，髑髅见梦曰："子之谈者似辩士。视子所言，皆生人之累也，死则无此矣。子欲闻死之说乎？"

庄子曰："然。"

髑髅曰："死，无君于上，无臣于下；亦无四时之事，从然以天地为春秋，虽南面王乐，不能过也。"

庄子不信，曰："吾使司命复生子形，为子骨肉肌肤，反子父母妻子闾里知识，子欲之乎？"

髑髅深矉蹙頞曰："吾安能弃南面王乐而复为人间之劳乎！"

《庄子◎至乐第十八》

P75-P76 昔者海鸟止于鲁郊，鲁侯御而觞之于庙，奏九韶以为乐，具太牢以为膳。鸟乃眩视忧悲，不敢食一脔，不敢饮一杯，三日而死。此以己养养鸟也，非以鸟养养鸟也。夫以鸟养养鸟者，宜栖之深林，游之坛陆，浮之江湖，食之鳅鯈，随行列而止，委蛇而处。彼唯人言之恶闻，奚以夫诡诡为乎！咸池九韶之乐，张之洞庭之野，鸟闻之而飞，兽闻之而走，鱼闻之而下入，人卒闻之，相与还而观之。鱼处水而生，人处水而死，彼必相与异，其好恶故异也。故先圣不一其能，不同其事。名止于实，义设于适，是之谓条达而福持。

《庄子◎至乐第十八》

P77 夫醉者之坠车，虽疾不死。骨节与人同而犯害与人异，其神全也，乘亦不知也，坠亦不知也，死生惊惧不入乎其胸中，是故遻物而不慑。彼得全于酒而犹若是，而况得全于天乎？

《庄子◎达生第十九》

P78-P79 庄子行于山中，见大木，枝叶盛茂，伐木者止其旁而不取也。问其故，曰："无所可用。"庄子曰："此木以不材得终其天年。"

夫子出于山，舍于故人之家。故人喜，命竖子杀雁而烹之。竖子请曰："其一能鸣，其一不能鸣，请奚杀？"主人曰："杀不能鸣者。"

明日，弟子问于庄子曰："昨日山中之木，以不材得终其天年；今主人之雁，以不材死；先生将何处？"

庄子笑曰："周将处乎材与不材之间。材与不材之间，似之而非也，故未免乎累。若夫乘道德而浮游则不然。无誉无訾，一龙一蛇，与时俱化，而无肯专为；一上一下，以和为量，浮游乎万物之祖；物物而不物于物，则故可得而累邪！此神农黄帝之法则也。若夫万物之情，人伦之传，则不然。合则离，成则毁；廉则挫，尊则议，有为则亏，贤则谋，不肖则欺，故可得而必乎哉！悲夫！弟子志之，其唯道德之乡乎！"

《庄子◎山木第二十》

P80-P81 孔子围于陈蔡之间，七日不火食。

大公任往吊之曰："子几死乎？"曰："然。"

"子恶死乎？"曰："然。"

任曰："予尝言不死之道。东海有鸟焉，其名曰意怠。其为鸟也，翂翂翐翐，而似无能；引援而飞，迫胁而栖；进不敢为前，退不敢为后；食不敢先尝，必取其绪。是故其行列不斥，而外人卒不得害，是以免于患。直木先伐，甘井先竭。子其意者饰知以惊愚，修身以明污，昭昭乎如揭日月而行，故不免也。昔吾闻之大成之人曰：'自伐者无功，功成者堕，名成者亏。'孰能去功与名而还与众人！道流而不明，居得而不名处；纯纯常常，乃比于狂；削迹捐势，不为功名，是故无责于人，人亦无责焉。至人不闻，子何喜哉！"

孔子曰："善哉！"辞其交游，去其弟子，逃于大泽；衣裘褐，食杼栗，入兽不乱群，入鸟不乱行。鸟兽不恶，而况人乎！

《庄子◎山木第二十》

P82 子独不闻假人之亡与？林回弃千金之璧，负赤子而趋。或曰："为其布与？赤子之布寡矣；为其累与？赤子之累多矣；弃千金之璧，负赤子而趋，何也？"林回曰："彼以利合，此以天属也。"夫以利合者,迫穷祸患害相弃也;以天属者,迫穷祸患害相收也。夫相收之与相弃亦远矣。

《庄子◎山木第二十》

P83 "何谓无受人益难?"

仲尼曰:"始用四达,爵禄并至而不穷,物之所利,乃非己也,吾命其在外者也。君子不为盗,贤人不为窃。吾若取之,何哉!故曰,鸟莫知于鹢鹢,目之所不宜处,不给视,虽落其实,弃之而走。其畏人也,而袭诸人间,社稷存焉尔。"

《庄子◎山木第二十》

P84-P85 庄周游于雕陵之樊,睹一异鹊自南方来者,翼广七尺,目大运寸,感周之颡而集于栗林。庄周曰:"此何鸟哉,翼殷不逝,目大不睹?"蹇裳躩步,执弹而留之。睹一蝉,方得美荫而忘其身;螳螂执翳而搏之,见得而忘其形;异鹊从而利之,见利而忘其真。庄周怵然曰:"噫!物固相累,二类相召也!"捐弹而反走,虞人逐而诮之。

庄周反入,三日不庭。蔺且从而问之:"夫子何为顷间甚不庭乎?"

庄周曰:"吾守形而忘身,观于浊水而迷于清渊。且吾闻诸夫子曰:'入其俗,从其令,'今吾游于雕陵而忘吾身,异鹊感吾颡,游于栗林而忘真,栗林虞人以吾为戮,吾所以不庭也。"

《庄子◎山木第二十》

P86 楚王与凡君坐,少焉,楚王左右曰凡亡者三。凡君曰:"凡之亡也,不足以丧吾存。夫'凡之亡不足以丧吾存',则楚之存不足以存存。由是观之,则凡未始亡而楚未始存也。"

《庄子◎田子方第二十一》

P87-P88 知北游于玄水之上,登隐弅之丘,而适遭无为谓焉。知谓无为谓曰:"予欲有问乎若:何思何虑则知道?何处何服则安道?何从何道则得道?"三问而无为谓不答也,非不答,不知答也。

知不得问,反于白水之南,登狐阕之上,而睹狂屈焉。知以之言也问乎狂屈。

狂屈曰:"唉!予所欲言。"

知不得问,反于帝宫,见黄帝而问焉。黄帝曰:"无思无虑始知道,无处无服始安道,无从无道始得道。"

知问黄帝曰:"我与若知之,彼与彼不知也,其孰是邪?"

黄帝曰:"彼无为谓真是也,狂屈似之;我与汝终不近也。夫知者不言,言者不知,故圣人行不言之教。道不可致,德不可至。仁可为也,义可亏也,礼相伪也。故曰,'失道而后德,失德而后仁,失仁而后义,失义而后礼。礼者,道之华而乱之首也。'故曰,'为道者日损,损之又损之以至于无为,无为而无不为也。'今已为物也,欲复归根,不亦难乎!其易也,其唯大人乎!"

《庄子◎知北游第二十二》

P89 老聃之役有庚桑楚者,偏得老聃之道,以北居畏垒之山,其臣之画然知者去之,其妾之挈然仁者远之;拥肿之与居,鞅掌之为使。居三年,畏垒大壤。畏垒之民相与言曰:"庚桑楚之始来,吾洒然异之,今吾日计之而不足,岁计之而有余。庶几其圣人乎!子胡不相与尸而祝之,社而稷之乎?"

庚桑子闻之,南面而不释然。弟子异之。庚桑子曰:"弟子何异于予?夫春气发而百草生,正得秋而万宝成。夫春与秋，岂无得而然哉？天道已行矣。吾闻至人，尸居环堵之室，而百姓猖狂不知所如往。今以畏垒之细民而窃窃焉欲俎豆予于贤人之间，我其杓之人邪！吾是以不释于老聃之言。"

《庄子◎庚桑楚第二十三》

P90-P91 黄帝将见大隗乎具茨之山，方明为御，昌㝢骖乘，张若謵朋前马，昆阍滑稽后车；至于襄城之野，七圣皆迷，无所问涂。

适遇牧马童子，问涂焉，曰："若知具茨之山乎？"曰："然。"

"若知大隗之所存乎？"曰："然。"

黄帝曰："异哉小童！非徒知具茨之山，又知大隗之所存。请问为天下。"

小童曰："夫为天下者，亦若此而已矣，又奚事焉！予少而自游于六合之内，予适有瞀病，有长者教予曰：'若乘日之车而游于襄城之野。'今予病少痊，予又且后游于六合之外。夫为天下亦若此而已，予又奚事焉！"

黄帝曰："夫为天下者，则诚非吾子之事。虽然，请问为天下。"小童辞。黄帝又问。小童曰："夫为天下者，亦奚以异乎牧马者哉！亦去其害马者而已矣！"

黄帝再拜稽首，称天师而退。

《庄子◎徐无鬼第二十四》

P92-P93 庄子送葬，过惠子之墓，顾谓从者曰："郢人垩慢其鼻端若蝇翼，使匠石斲之。匠石运斤成风，听而斲之，尽垩而鼻不伤，郢人立不失容。"

"宋元君闻之，召匠石曰：'尝试为寡人为之。'匠石曰：'臣则尝能斲之。虽然，臣之质死久矣。'自夫子之死也，吾无以为质矣，吾无与言之矣。"

《庄子◎徐无鬼第二十四》

P94 "有国于蜗之左角者曰触氏，有国于蜗之右角者曰蛮氏，时相与争地而战，伏尸数万，逐北旬有五日而后反。"

君曰："噫！其虚言与？"

曰："臣请为君实之。君以意在四方上下有穷乎？"君曰："无穷。"……

曰："通达之中有魏，于魏中有梁，于梁中有王，王与蛮氏，有辩乎？"君曰："无辩。"

客出而君惝然若有亡也。

《庄子◎则阳第二十五》

P95 庄周家贫，故往贷粟于监河侯。监河侯曰："诺。我将得邑金，将贷子三百金，可乎？"

庄周忿然作色曰："周昨来，有中道而呼者。周顾视车辙中，有鲋鱼焉。周问之曰：'鲋鱼来！子何为者邪？'对曰：'我，东海之波臣也。君岂有斗升之水而活我哉？'周曰：'诺。我且南游吴越之王，激西江之水而迎子，可乎？'鲋鱼忿然作色曰：'吾失我常与，我无所处。吾得斗升之水然活耳，居乃言此，曾不如早索我于枯鱼之肆！'"

《庄子◎外物第二十六》

P96-P97 宋元君夜半而梦人被发窥阿门，曰："予自宰路之渊，予为清江使河伯之所，渔者余且得予。"

元君觉，使人占之，曰："此神龟也。"
君曰："渔者有余且乎？"
左右曰："有。"
君曰："令余且会朝。"
明日，余且朝。君曰："渔何得？"
对曰："且之网得白龟焉，其圆五尺。"
君曰："献若之龟。"龟至，君再欲杀之，再欲活之，心疑，卜之，曰："杀龟以卜吉。"乃刳龟，七十二钻而无遗筴。仲尼曰："神龟能见梦于元君，而不能避余且之网；知能七十二钻而无遗筴，不能避刳肠之患。如是，则知有所困，神有所不及也。虽有至知，万人谋之。鱼不畏网而畏鹈鹕。去小知而大知明，去善而自善矣。婴儿生无石师而能言，与能言者处也。"

《庄子◎外物第二十六》

P98 惠子谓庄子曰："子言无用。"
庄子曰："知无用而始可与言用矣。天地非不广且大也，人之所用容足耳。然则厕足而垫之致黄泉，人尚有用乎？"
惠子曰："无用。"
庄子曰："然则无用之为用也亦明矣。"

《庄子◎外物第二十六》

P99 荃者所以在鱼，得鱼而忘荃；蹄者所以在兔，得兔而忘蹄；言者所以在意，得意而忘言。吾安得夫忘言之人而与之言哉！

《庄子◎外物第二十六》

P100 阳子居南之沛，老聃西游于秦，邀于郊，至于梁而遇老子。老子中道仰天而叹曰："始以汝为可教，今不可也。"
阳子居不答。至舍，进盥漱巾栉，脱屦户外，膝行而前曰："向者弟子欲请夫子，夫子行不闲，是以不敢，今闲矣，请问其过。"
老子曰："而睢睢盱盱，而谁与居！大白若辱，盛德若不足。"阳子居蹴然变容曰："敬闻命矣！"
其往也，舍者迎将，其家公执席，妻执巾栉，舍者避席，炀者避灶，其反也，舍者与之争席矣。

《庄子◎寓言第二十七》

P101-P102 原宪居鲁，环堵之室，茨以生草，蓬户不完，桑以为枢；而瓮牖二室，褐以为塞；上漏下湿，匡坐而弦。
子贡乘大马，中绀而表素，轩车不容巷，往见原宪。原宪华冠纵履，杖藜而应门。
子贡曰："嘻！先生何病？"
原宪应之曰："宪闻之，无财谓之贫，学而不能行谓之病。今宪，贫也，非病也。"
子贡逡巡而有愧色。
原宪笑曰："夫希世而行，比周而友，学以为人，教以为己，仁义之慝，舆马之饰，宪不忍为也。"

《庄子◎让王第二十八》

P103-P107 孔子与柳下季为友，柳下季之弟，名曰盗跖。盗跖从卒九千人，横行天下，侵暴诸侯，穴室枢户，驱人牛马，取人妇女，贪得忘亲，不顾父母兄弟，不祭先祖。所过之邑，大国守城，小国入保，万民苦之。

孔子谓柳下季曰："夫为人父者，必能诏其子；为人兄者，必能教其弟。若父不能诏其子，兄不能教其弟，则无贵父子兄弟之亲矣。今先生，世之才士也，弟为盗跖，为天下害，而弗能教也，丘窃为先生羞之。丘请为先生往说之。"

柳下季曰："先生言为人父者必能诏其子，为人兄者必能教其弟，若子不听父之诏，弟不受兄之教，虽今先生之辩，将奈之何哉！且跖之为人也，心如涌泉，意如飘风，强足以距敌，辩足以饰非，顺其心则喜，逆其心则怒，易辱人以言。先生必无往。"

孔子不听，颜回为驭，子贡为右，往见盗跖。盗跖乃方休卒徒大山之阳，脍人肝而铺之。孔子下车而前，见谒者曰："鲁人孔丘，闻将军高义，敬再拜谒者。"

……

孔子曰："丘闻之，凡天下有三德：生而长大，美好无双，少长贵贱见而皆说之，此上德也；知维天地，能辩诸物，此中德也；勇悍果敢，聚众率兵，此下德也。凡人有此一德者，足以南面称孤矣。今将军兼此三者，身长八尺二寸，面目有光，唇如激丹，齿如齐贝，音中黄钟，而名曰盗跖，丘窃为将军耻不取焉。将军有意听臣，臣请南使吴越，北使齐鲁，东使宋卫，西使晋楚，使为将军造大城数百里，立数十万户之邑，尊将军为诸侯，与天下更始，罢兵休卒，收养昆弟，共祭先祖。此圣人才士之行，而天下之愿也。"

盗跖大怒曰："丘来前！夫可规以利而可谏以言者，皆愚陋恒民之谓耳。今长大美好，人见而悦之者，此吾父母之遗德也。丘虽不吾誉，吾独不自知邪？且吾闻之，好面誉人者，亦好背而毁之。今丘告我以大城众民，是欲规我以利而恒民畜我也，安可久长也！城之大者，莫大乎天下矣。尧舜有天下，子孙无置锥之地；汤武立为天子，而后世绝灭；非以其利大故邪？"

孔子再拜趋走，出门上车，执辔三失，目芒然无见，色若死灰，据轼低头，不能出气。归到鲁东门外，适遇柳下季。柳下季曰："今者阙然数日不见，车马有行色，得微往见跖邪？"

孔子仰天而叹曰："然。"

柳下季曰："跖得无逆汝意若前乎？"

孔子曰："然。丘所谓无病而自灸也，疾走料虎头，编虎须，几不免虎口哉！"

《庄子◎盗跖第二十九》

P108-P114 昔赵文王喜剑，剑士夹门而客三千余人，日夜相击于前，死伤者岁百余人，好之不厌。如是三年，国衰，诸侯谋之。

太子悝患之，募左右曰："孰能说王之意止剑士者，赐之千金。"左右曰："庄子当能。"

太子乃使人以千金奉庄子。庄子弗受，与使者俱，往见太子曰："太子何以教周，赐周千金？芽"

太子曰："闻夫子明圣，谨奉千金以币从者。夫子弗受，悝尚何敢言！"

庄子曰："闻太子所欲用周者，欲绝王之喜好也。使臣上说大王而逆王意，下不当太子，则身刑而死，周尚安所事金乎？使臣上说大王，下当太子，赵国何求而不得也！"

太子曰："然。吾王所见，唯剑士也。"

庄子曰："诺。周善为剑。"

太子曰："然吾王所见剑士，皆蓬头突鬓垂冠，曼胡之缨，短后之衣，瞋目而语难，王乃说之。今夫子必儒服而见王，事必大逆。"

庄子曰："请治剑服。"治剑服三日，乃见太子。太子乃与见王，王脱白刃待之。庄子入殿门不趋，见王不拜。

王曰："子欲何以教寡人，使太子先焉？"

曰："臣闻大王喜剑，故以剑见王。"

王曰："子之剑何能禁制？"

曰："臣之剑，十步一人，千里不留行。"

王大悦之，曰："天下无敌矣！"

庄子曰："夫为剑者，示之以虚，开之以利，后之以发，先之以至。愿得试之。"

王曰："夫子休就舍，待命令设戏请夫子。"

王乃校剑士七日，死伤者六十余人，得五六人，使奉剑于殿下，乃召庄子。王曰："今日试使士敦剑。"

庄子曰："望之久矣。"

王曰："夫子所御杖，长短何如？"

曰："臣之所奉皆可。然臣有三剑，唯王所用，请先言而后试。"

王曰："愿闻三剑。"

曰："有天子剑，有诸侯剑，有庶人剑。"

王曰："天子之剑何如？"

曰："天子之剑，以燕谿石城为锋，齐岱为锷，晋魏为脊，周宋为镡，韩魏为夹；包以四夷，裹以四时；绕以渤海，带以恒山；制以五行，论以刑德；开以阴阳，持以春夏，行以秋冬。此剑，直之无前，举之无上，案之无下，运之无旁，上决浮云，下绝地纪。此剑一用，匡诸侯，天下服矣。此天子之剑也。"

文王芒然自失，曰："诸侯之剑何如？"

曰："诸侯之剑，以知勇士为锋，以清廉士为锷，以贤良士为脊，以忠圣士为镡，以豪杰士为夹。此剑，直之亦无前，举之亦无上，案之亦无下，运之亦无旁；上法圆天以顺三光，下法方地以顺四时，中和民意以安四乡。此剑一用，如雷霆之震也，四封之内，无不宾服而听从君命者矣。此诸侯之剑也。"

王曰："庶人之剑何如？"

曰："庶人之剑，蓬头突鬓垂冠，曼胡之缨，短后之衣，瞋目而语难。相击于前，上斩颈领，下决肝肺。此庶人之剑，无异于斗鸡，一旦命已绝矣，无所用于国事。今大王有天子之位而好庶人之剑，臣窃为大王薄之。"

王乃牵而上殿。宰人上食，王三环之。庄子曰："大王安坐定气，剑事已毕奏矣。"

于是文王不出宫三月，剑士皆服毙其处也。

《庄子○说剑第三十》

P115-P117　孔子游乎缁帷之林，休坐乎杏坛之上。弟子读书，孔子弦歌鼓琴，奏曲未半。有渔父者，下船而来，须眉交白，被发揄袂，行原以上，距陆而止，左手据膝，右手持颐以听。曲终而招子贡子路，二人俱对。

客指孔子曰："彼何为者也？"

子路对曰："鲁之君子也。"

客问其族。子路对曰："族孔氏。"

客曰："孔氏者何治也？"

子路未应，子贡对曰："孔氏者，性服忠信，身行仁义，饰礼乐，选人伦，上以忠于世主，下以化于齐民，将以利天下。此孔氏之所治也。"

又问曰:"有土之君与?"

子贡曰:"非也。"

"侯王之佐与?"

子贡曰:"非也。"……

孔子再拜而起曰:"丘少而修学,以至于今,六十九岁矣,无所得闻至教,敢不虚心!"

客曰:"……且人有八疵,事有四患,不可不察也。非其事而事之,谓之总;莫之顾而进之,谓之佞;希意道言,谓之谄;不择是非而言,谓之谀;好言人之恶,谓之谗;析交离亲,谓之贼;称誉诈伪以败恶人,谓之慝;不择善否,两容颊适,偷拔其所欲,谓之险。此八疵者,外以乱人,内以伤身,君子不友,明君不臣。所谓四患者:好经大事,变更易常,以挂功名,谓之叨;专知擅事,侵人自用,谓之贪;见过不更,闻谏愈甚,谓之狠;人同于己则可,不同于己,虽善不善,谓之矜。此四患也。能去八疵,无行四患,而始可教已。"

《庄子◎渔父第三十一》

P118 人有畏影恶迹而去之走者;举足愈数而迹愈多,走愈疾而影不离身,自以为尚迟,疾走不休,绝力而死。不知处阴以休影,处静以息迹,愚亦甚矣!

《庄子◎渔父第三十一》

P120 巧者劳而知者忧,无能者无所求,饱食而敖游,汎若不系之舟,虚而敖游者也。

《庄子◎列御寇第三十二》

P121 朱泙漫学屠龙于支离益,单千金之家,三年技成而无所用其巧。

《庄子◎列御寇第三十二》

P123-P124 人有见宋王者,锡车十乘,以其十乘骄稚庄子。

庄子曰:"河上有家贫恃纬萧而食者,其子没于渊,得千金之珠。其父谓其子曰:'取石来锻之!夫千金之珠,必在九重之渊而骊龙颔下,子能得珠者,必遭其睡也。使骊龙而寤,子尚奚微之有哉!'"

"今宋国之深,非直九重之渊也;宋王之猛,非直骊龙也;子能得车者,必遭其睡也。使宋王而寤,子为齑粉夫!"

《庄子◎列御寇第三十二》

P125 或聘于庄子。庄子应其使曰:"子见夫牺牛乎?衣以文绣,食以刍叔,及其牵而入于大庙,虽欲为孤犊,其可得乎!"

《庄子◎列御寇第三十二》

P126 庄子将死,弟子欲厚葬之。庄子曰:"吾以天地为棺椁,以日月为连璧,星辰为珠玑,万物为赍送。吾葬具岂不备邪?何以加此!"

弟子曰:"吾恐乌鸢之食夫子也。"

庄子曰:"在上为乌鸢食,在下为蝼蚁食,夺彼与此,何其偏也!"

《庄子◎列御寇第三十二》

P127-P129 庄子书,据汉志说有五十二篇,未受重视。至唐玄宗时代,始渐器重,被列入经书。

现存为晋郭象所重编的三十三篇。即:"内篇"七篇——逍遥游、齐物论、养生主、人间世、德充符、大宗师、应帝王;"外篇"十五篇——骈拇、马蹄、胠箧、在宥、天地、天道、天运、刻意、缮性、秋水、至乐、达生、山木、田子方、知北游;"杂篇"十一篇——庚桑楚、徐无鬼、则阳、外物、寓言、让王、盗跖、说剑、渔父、列御寇、天下。注者甚多,以唐郭象注本及清王先谦的庄子集解较佳。

庄子名叫周,是宋国蒙地人。他曾做过蒙地漆园的官吏,跟梁惠王、齐宣王同时代。

庄子的学问非常渊博,研究的范围无所不包,庄子之学,其要本归老子,可谓集道家之大成。他的哲理,对自然与人生有许多宝贵的启示。

他的个性恬淡寡欲,不慕名利,楚威王闻知庄周贤能,遣使者带着重金币去聘请他,请他做卿相,却遭他婉辞拒绝。

北冥有鱼,其名为鲲。鲲之大,不知其几千里也;化而为鸟,其名为鹏。鹏之背,不知其几千里也;怒而飞,其翼若垂天之云。是鸟也,海运则将徙于南冥。南冥者,天池也。

齐谐者,志怪者也。谐之言曰:"鹏之徙于南冥也,水击三千里,抟扶摇而上者九万里。去以六月息者也。"野马也,尘埃也,生物之以息相吹也。天之苍苍,其正色邪?其远而无所至极邪?其视下也,亦若是则已矣。

《庄子◎逍遥游第一》

P130 夫列子御风而行,泠然善也,旬有五日而后反。彼于致福者,未数数然也。此虽免乎行,犹有所待者也。

若夫乘天地之正,而御六气之辩,以游无穷者,彼且恶乎待哉!

故曰,至人无己,神人无功,圣人无名。

《庄子◎逍遥游第一》

P131 尧让天下于许由,曰:"日月出矣,而爝火不息,其于光也,不亦难乎!时雨降矣,而犹浸灌,其于泽也,不亦劳乎!夫子立,而天下治,而我犹尸之,吾自视缺然。请致天下。"

许由曰:"子治天下,天下既已治也。而我犹代子,吾将为名乎?名者实之宾也。吾将为宾乎?鹪鹩巢于深林,不过一枝;偃鼠饮河,不过满腹。归休乎君,予无所用天下为!庖人虽不治庖,尸祝不越樽俎而代之矣。"

《庄子◎逍遥游第一》

P132 百骸、九窍、六藏,赅而存焉,吾谁与为亲?汝皆说之乎?其有私焉?如是皆有为臣妾乎?其臣妾不足以相治乎?其递相为君臣乎?其有真君存焉?如求得其情与不得,无益损乎其真。

一受其成形,不化以待尽。与物相刃相靡,其行进如驰,而莫之能止,不亦悲乎!终身役役而不见其成功,苶然疲役而不知其所归,可不哀邪!人谓之不死,奚益!其形化,其心与之然,可不谓大哀乎?人之生也,固若是芒乎?其我独芒,而人亦有不芒者乎?

《庄子◎齐物论第二》

P133 今且有言于此,不知其与是类乎?其与是不类乎?类与不类,相与为类,则与彼无以异矣。虽然,请尝言之。有始也者,有未始有始也者,有未始有夫未始有始也者。有"有"也者,有"无"

也者,有未始有无也者,有未始有夫未始有无也者。俄而有无矣,而未知有无之果孰有孰无也。今我则已有谓矣,而未知吾所谓之其果有谓乎,其果无谓乎?

《庄子◎齐物论第二》

P134 故昔者尧问于舜曰:"我欲伐宗、脍、胥敖,南面而不释然。其故何也?"舜曰:"夫三子者,犹存乎蓬艾之间。若不释然,何哉?昔者十日并出,万物皆照,而况德之进乎日者乎!"

《庄子◎齐物论第二》

P135 吾生也有涯,而知也无涯。以有涯随无涯,殆已;已而为知者,殆而已矣。为善无近名,为恶无近刑。缘督以为经,可以保身,可以全生,可以养亲,可以尽年。

《庄子◎养生主第三》

P136 公文轩见右师而惊曰:"是何人也?恶乎介也?天与,其人与?"曰:"天也,非人也,天之生是使独也,人之貌有与也。以是知其天也,非人也。"

《庄子◎养生主第三》

P137 老聃死,秦失吊之,三号而出。弟子曰:"非夫子之友邪?"
曰:"然。"
"然则吊焉若此,可乎?"
曰:"然。始也吾以为至人也,而今非也。向吾入而吊焉,有老者哭之,如哭其子;少者哭之,如哭其母。彼其所以会之,必有不蕲言而言,不蕲哭而哭者。是遁天倍情,忘其所受,古者谓之遁天之刑。适来,夫子时也;适去,夫子顺也。安时而处顺,哀乐不能入也,古者谓是帝之悬解。"

《庄子◎养生主第三》

P138 颜回见仲尼,请行。曰:"奚之?"曰:"将之卫。"曰:"奚为焉?"曰:"回闻卫君,其年壮,其行独,轻用其国,而不见其过……吾无以进矣,敢问其方。"仲尼曰:"斋,吾将语若!有心而为之,其易邪?易之者,皞天不宜。"颜回曰:"回之家贫,惟不饮酒不茹荤者数月矣。如此,则可以为斋乎?"曰:"是祭祀之斋,非心斋也。"回曰:"敢问心斋。"
仲尼曰:"若一志,无听之以耳而听之以心,无听之以心而听之以气!耳止于听,心止于符。气也者,虚而待物者也。惟道集虚。虚者,心斋也。"

《庄子◎人间世第四》

P139 叶公子高将使于齐,问于仲尼曰:"王使诸梁也甚重,齐之待使者,盖将甚敬而不急。匹夫犹未可动,而况诸侯乎!吾甚栗之……"
仲尼曰:"天下有大戒二:其一,命也;其一,义也。子之爱亲,命也,不可解于心;臣之事君,义也,无适而非君也,无所逃于天地之间。是之谓大戒,是以夫事其亲者,不择地而安之,孝之至也;夫事其君者,不择事而安之,忠之盛也……为人臣子者,固有所不得已。行事之情而忘其身,何暇至于悦生而恶死!夫子其行可矣……"

《庄子◎人间世第四》

P140 孔子适楚，楚狂接舆游其门曰："凤兮凤兮，何如德之衰也！来世不可待，往世不可追也。天下有道，圣人成焉；天下无道，圣人生焉。方今之时，仅免刑焉。福轻乎羽，莫之知载；祸重乎地，莫之知避。已乎已乎，临人以德！殆乎殆乎，画地而趋！迷阳迷阳，无伤吾行！郤曲郤曲，无伤吾足！"

《庄子◎人间世第四》

P141 仲尼曰："丘也尝使于楚矣，适见㹠子食于其死母者，少焉眴若皆弃之而走。不见己焉尔，不得类焉尔。所爱其母者，非爱其形也，爱使其形者也。"

《庄子◎德充符第五》

P142 惠子谓庄子曰："人故无情乎？"庄子曰："然。"惠子曰："人而无情，何以谓之人？"庄子曰："道与之貌，天与之形，恶得不谓之人？"惠子曰："既谓之人，恶得无情？"庄子曰："是非吾所谓情也。吾所谓无情者，言人之不以好恶内伤其身，常因自然而不益生也。"

《庄子◎德充符第五》

P143 且有真人而后有真知。何谓真人？古之真人，不逆寡，不雄成，不谟士。若然者，过而弗悔，当而不自得也，若然者，登高不栗，入水不濡，入火不热。是知之能登假于道者也若此。

《庄子◎大宗师第六》

P144 死生，命也，其有夜旦之常，天也。人之有所不得与，皆物之情也。彼特以天为父，而身犹爱之，而况其卓乎！人特以有君为愈乎己，而身犹死之，而况其真乎！

《庄子◎大宗师第六》

P145 泉涸，鱼相与处于陆，相呴以湿，相濡以沫，不如相忘于江湖，与其誉尧而非桀也，不如两忘而化其道。

《庄子◎大宗师第六》

P146 夫藏舟于壑，藏山于泽，谓之固矣。然而夜半有力者负之而走，昧者不知也。藏小大有宜，犹有所遁。若夫藏天下于天下而不得所遁，是恒物之大情也。特犯人之形而犹喜之。若人之形者，万化而未始有极也，其为乐可胜计邪！故圣人将游于物之所不得遁而皆存。善夭善老，善始善终，人犹效之，又况万物之所系，而一化之所待乎！

《庄子◎大宗师第六》

P147-P148 意而子见许由。许由曰："尧何以资汝？"
意而子曰："尧谓我：'汝必躬服仁义而明言是非。'"许由曰："而奚来为轵？夫尧既已黥汝以仁义，而劓汝以是非矣，汝将何以游夫遥荡恣睢转徙之涂乎？"
意而子曰："虽然，吾愿游于其藩。"许由曰："不然。夫盲者无以与乎眉目颜色之好，瞽者无以与乎青黄黼黻之观。"意而子曰："夫无庄之失其美，据梁之失其力，黄帝之亡其知，皆在炉捶之间耳。庸讵知夫造物者之不息我黥而补我劓，使我乘成以随先生邪？"
许由曰："噫！未可知也。我为汝言大略。吾师乎！吾师乎！鳌万物而不为戾，泽及万世而不为仁，长于上古而不为老，覆载天地刻雕众形而不为巧。此所游已。"

庄子说 自然的箫声

《庄子◎大宗师第六》

P149-P150 颜回曰:"回益矣。"仲尼曰:"何谓也?"曰:"回忘礼乐矣。"曰:"可矣,犹未也。"他日,复见,曰:"回益矣。"曰:"何谓也?"曰:"回忘仁义矣。"曰:"可矣,犹未也。"他日,复见,曰:"回益矣。"曰:"何谓也?"曰:"回坐忘矣。"仲尼蹴然曰:"何谓坐忘?"颜回曰:"堕肢体,黜聪明,离形去知,同于大通,此谓坐忘。"仲尼曰:"同则无好也,化则无常也。而果其贤乎!丘也请从而后也。明,离形去知,同于大通,此谓坐忘。"仲尼曰:"同则无好也,化则无常也。而果其贤乎!丘也请从而后也。"

《庄子◎大宗师第六》

P151 无为名尸,无为谋府;无为事任,无为知主。体尽无穷,而游无朕;尽其所受乎天,而无见得,亦虚而已。至人之用心若镜,不将不迎,应而不藏,故能胜物而不伤。

《庄子◎应帝王第七》

P152 南海之帝为儵,北海之帝为忽,中央之帝为浑沌。儵与忽时相与遇于浑沌之地,浑沌待之甚善。儵与忽谋报浑沌之德,曰:"人皆有七窍,以视听食息,此独无有,尝试凿之。"日凿一窍,七日而浑沌死。

《庄子◎应帝王第七》

P153 骈拇枝指,出乎性哉!而侈于德。附赘县疣,出乎形哉!则侈于性。多方乎仁义而用之者,列于五藏哉!而非道德之正也。是故骈于足者,连无用之肉也;枝于手者,树无用之指也;骈枝于五藏之情者,淫僻于仁义之行,而多方于聪明之用也。

《庄子◎应帝王第八》

P154 夫小惑易方,大惑易性。何以知其然邪?有虞氏招仁义以挠天下也,天下莫不奔命于仁义,是非以仁义易其性与?故尝试论之,自三代以下者,天下莫不以物易其性矣。小人则以身殉利,士则以身殉名,大夫则以身殉家,圣人则以身殉天下。故此数子者,事业不同,名声异号,其于伤性以身为殉,一也。

《庄子◎骈拇第八》

P155-P156 马,蹄可以践霜雪,毛可以御风寒,龁草饮水,翘足而陆,此马之真性也。虽有义台路寝,无所用之。及至伯乐,曰:"我善治马。"烧之,剔之,刻之,雒之,连之以羁馽,编之以皂栈,马之死者十二三矣;饥之,渴之,驰之,骤之,整之,齐之,前有橛饰之患,而后有鞭笑之威,而马之死者已过半矣。陶者曰:"我善治埴,圆者中规,方者中矩。"匠人曰:"我善治木,曲者中钩,直者应绳。"夫埴木之性,岂欲中规矩钩绳哉?然且世世称之曰"伯乐善治马,而陶匠善治埴木",此亦治天下者之过也。

《庄子◎马蹄第九》

P157 夫赫胥氏之时,民居不知所为,行不知所之,含哺而熙,鼓腹而游,民能以此矣。及至圣人,屈折礼乐以匡天下之形,县跂仁义以慰天下之心,而民乃始踶跂好知,争归于利,不可止也。此亦圣人之过也。

《庄子◎马蹄第九》

P158 将为胠箧探囊发匮之盗而为守备，则必摄缄縢固扃，此世俗之所谓知也。然而巨盗至，则负匮揭箧担囊而趋，唯恐缄縢扃镝之不固也。然则乡之所谓知者，不乃为大盗积者也？

故尝试论之，世俗之所谓知者，有不为大盗积者乎？所谓圣者，有不为大盗守者乎？何以知其然邪？

《庄子◎胠箧第十》

P159 黄帝游乎赤水之北，登乎昆仑之丘而南望，还归遗其玄珠。使知索之而不得，使离朱索之而不得，使吃诟索之而不得也。

乃使象罔，象罔得之。黄帝曰："异哉！象罔乃可以得之乎？"

《庄子◎天地第十二》

P161 天道运而无所积，故万物成；帝道运而无所积，故天下归，圣道运而无所积，故海内服。明于天，通于圣，六通四辟于帝王之德者，其自为也，昧然无不静者矣。圣人之静也，非曰静也善，故静也；万物无足以铙心者，故静也。水静则明烛须眉，平中准，大匠取法焉。水静犹明，而况精神，圣人之心静乎！天地之鉴也，万物之镜也。夫虚静恬淡寂漠无为者，天地之本，而道德之至，故帝王圣人休焉。

《庄子◎天道第十三》

P162 昔者舜问于尧曰："天王之用心何如？"尧曰："吾不敖无告，不废穷民，苦死者，嘉孺子而哀妇人。此吾所以用心已。"舜曰："美则美矣，而未大也。"尧曰："然则何如？"舜曰："天德而土宁，日月照而四时行，若昼夜之有经，云行而雨施矣。"尧曰："胶胶扰扰乎！子，天之合也；我，人之合也。"夫天地者，古之所大也，而黄帝尧舜之所共美也，故古之王天下者，奚为哉？天地而已矣。

《庄子◎天道第十三》

P163-P164 刻意尚行，离世异俗，高论怨诽，为亢而已矣；此山谷之士，非世之人，枯槁赴渊者之所好也。语仁义忠信，恭俭推让为修而已矣；此平世之士，教诲之人，游居学者之所好也。语大功，立大名，礼君臣，正上下，为治而已矣；此朝廷之士，尊主强国之人，致功并兼者之所好也。就薮泽，处闲旷，钓鱼闲处，无为而已矣；此江海之士，避世之人，间暇者之所好也。吹呴呼吸，吐故纳新，能经鸟申，为寿而已矣；此导引之士，养形之人，彭祖寿考者之所好也。

若夫不刻意而高，无仁义而修，无功名而治，无江海而闲，不导引而寿，无不忘也，无不有也，澹然无极而众美从之。此天地之道，圣人之德也。

《庄子◎刻意第十五》

P165 故曰，形劳而不休则弊，精用而不已则竭。水之性，不杂则清，莫动则平；郁闭而不流，亦不能清；天德之象也。故曰，纯粹而不杂，静一而不变，惔而无为，动而天行，此养神之道也。夫有干越之剑者，柙而藏之，不轻敢用也，宝之至也。精神四达并流，无所不极，上际于天，下蟠于地，化育万物，不可为象，其名为同帝。

《庄子◎刻意第十五》

P166 古之所谓隐士者，非伏身而弗见也，非闭其言而不出也，非藏其知而不发也，时命大谬也！当时命而大行乎天下，则反一无迹；不当时命而大穷乎天下，则深根宁极；此存身之道也。

《庄子◎缮性第十六》

P167-P168 秋水时至，百川灌河，泾流之大，两涘渚崖之间不辩牛马。于是焉河伯欣然自喜，以天下之美为尽在己。顺流而东行，至于北海，东面而视，不见水端，于是焉河伯始旋其面目，望洋向若而叹曰："野语有之曰：'闻道百以为莫己若者'，我之谓也。且夫我尝闻少仲尼之闻而轻伯夷之义者，始吾弗信；今我睹子之难穷也，吾非至于子之门，则殆矣，吾长见笑于大方之家。"

北海若曰："井龟不可以语于海者，拘于虚也；夏虫不可以语于冰者，笃于时也；曲士不可以语于道者，束于教也。今尔出于崖涘，观于大海，乃知尔丑，尔将可与语大理矣。天下之水，莫大于海，万川归之，不知何时止于不盈，尾闾泄之，不知何时已而不虚……计中国之在海内，不似稊米之在大仓乎？号物之数谓之万，人处一焉；人卒九州，谷食之所生，舟车之所通，人处一焉；此其比万物也，不似豪末之在于马体乎？五帝之所运，三王之所争，仁人之所忧，任士之所劳，尽此矣。伯夷辞之以为名，仲尼语之以为博，此其自多也，不似尔向之自多于水乎？"

《庄子◎秋水第十七》

P169 河伯曰："然则吾大天地而小（毫）末，可乎？"

北海若曰："否，夫物，量无穷，时无止，分无常，终始无故。是故大知观于远近，故小而不寡，大而不多，知量无穷；证曏今故，故遥而不闷，掇而不跂，知时无止；察乎盈虚，故得而不喜，失而不忧，知分之无常也；明乎坦涂，故生而不说，死而不祸，知终始之不可故也。……由此观之，又何（毫）以知末之足以定至细之倪，又以知天地之足以穷至大之域！"

《庄子◎秋水第十七》

P170 河伯曰："世之议者皆曰：'至精无形，至大不可围。'是信情乎？"

北海若曰："夫自细视大者不尽，自大视细者不明。故异便，此势之有也。夫精，小之微也；垺，大之殷也；夫精粗者，期于有形者也；无形者，数之所不能分也；不可围者，数之所不能穷也。可以言论者，物之粗也；可以意致者，物之精也；言之所不能论，意之所不能致者，不期精粗焉。"

《庄子◎秋水第十七》

P171 河伯曰："若物之外，若物之内，恶至而倪贵贱？恶至而倪小大？"

北海若曰："以道观之，物无贵贱；以物观之，自贵而相贱；以俗观之，贵贱不在己。以差观之，因其所大而大之，则万物莫不大；因其所小而小之，则万物莫不小；知天地之为稊米也，知毫末之为丘山也，则差数睹矣。以功观之，因其所有而有之，则万物莫不有；因其所无而无之；则万物莫不无；知东西之相反而不可以相无，则功分定矣。"

《庄子◎秋水第十七》

P172 河伯曰："然则我何为乎，何不为乎？吾辞受趣舍，吾终奈何？"

北海若曰："以道观之，何贵何贱，是谓反衍；无拘而志，与道大蹇。何少何多，是谓谢施。"

《庄子◎秋水第十七》

P173 河伯曰："然则何贵于道邪？"
北海若曰："知道者必达于理，达于理者必明于权，明于权者不以物害己。至德者，火弗能热，水弗能溺，寒暑弗能害，禽兽弗能贼。非谓其薄之也，言察乎安危，宁于祸福，谨于去就，莫之能害也。故曰，天在内，人在外，德在乎天。知乎人之行，本乎天，位乎得；蹢躅而屈伸，反要而语极。"

《庄子◎秋水第十七》

P174 庄子钓于濮水，楚王使大夫二人往先焉，曰："愿以境内累矣！"
庄子持竿不顾，曰："吾闻楚有神龟，死已三千岁矣，王以巾笥而藏之庙堂之上。此龟者，宁其死为留骨而贵乎？宁其生而曳尾于涂中乎？"
二大夫曰："宁生而曳尾于涂中。"
庄子曰："往矣！吾将曳尾于涂中。"

《庄子◎秋水第十七》

P175-P176 天下有至乐无有哉？有可以活身者无有哉？今奚为奚据？奚避奚处？奚就奚去？奚乐奚恶？
夫天下之所尊者，富贵寿善也；所乐者，身安厚味美服好色音声也；所下者，贫贱夭恶也；所苦者，身不得安逸，口不得厚味，形不得美服，目不得好色，耳不得音声；若不得者，则大忧以惧，其为形也，亦愚哉！

《庄子◎至乐第十八》

P177-P178 庄子妻死，惠子吊之，庄子则方箕踞鼓盆而歌。
惠子曰："与人居，长子、老、身死，不哭，亦足矣，又鼓盆而歌，不亦甚乎！"
庄子曰："不然。是其始死也，我独何能无概然！察其始而本无生，非徒无生也而本形，非徒无形也而本无气。杂乎芒芴之间，变而有气，气变而有形，形变而有生，今又变而之死，是相与为春秋冬夏四时行也。人且偃然寝于巨室，而我噭噭然随而哭之，自以为不通乎命，故止也。"

《庄子◎至乐第十八》

P179 支离叔与滑介叔观于冥伯之丘，昆仑之虚，黄帝之所休。俄而柳生其左肘，其意蹶蹶然恶之。
支离叔曰："子恶之乎？"
滑介叔曰："亡，予何恶！生者，假借也；假之而生生者，尘垢也。死生为昼夜。且吾与子观化而化及我，我又何恶焉！"

《庄子◎至乐第十八》

P180 列子行食于道从，见百岁髑髅，攓蓬而指之曰："唯予与汝知而未尝死，未尝生也。若果养乎？予果欢乎？"

《庄子◎至乐第十八》

P181 子列子问关尹曰："至人潜行不窒，蹈火不热，行乎万物之上而不栗。请问何以至于此？"
关尹曰："是纯气之守也，非知巧果敢之列。居，予语汝！凡有貌象声色者，皆物也，物与物何以相远？夫奚足以至乎先？是形色而已。则物之造乎不形而止乎无所化，夫得是而穷之者，物焉得而止焉！

彼将处乎不淫之度，而藏乎无端之纪，游乎万物之所终始，壹其性，养其气，合其德，以通乎物之所造。夫若是者，其天守全，其神无却，物奚自入焉！"

《庄子◎达生第十九》

P182-P183 仲尼适楚，出于林中，见佝偻者承蜩，犹掇之也。

仲尼曰："子巧乎！有道邪？"

曰："我有道也。五六月累丸二而不坠，则失者锱铢；累三而不坠，则失者十一；累五而不坠，犹掇之也。吾处身也，若橛株枸；吾执臂也，若槁木之枝；虽天地之大，万物之多，而唯蜩翼之知。吾不反不侧，不以万物易蜩之翼，何为而不得！"

孔子顾谓弟子曰："用志不分，乃凝于神，其佝偻丈人之谓乎！"

《庄子◎达生第十九》

P184-P185 颜渊问仲尼曰："吾尝济乎觞深之渊，津人操舟若神。吾问焉，曰：'操舟可学邪？'曰：'可。善游者数能。若乃夫没人，则未尝见舟而便操之也。'吾问焉而不吾告，敢问何谓也？"

仲尼曰："善游者数能，忘水也。若乃夫没人之未尝见舟而便操之也，彼视渊若陵，视舟之覆犹其车却也。覆却万方陈乎前而不得入其舍，恶往而不暇！以瓦注者巧，以钩注者惮，以黄金注者 。其巧一也，而有所矜，则重外也。凡外重者内拙。"

《庄子◎达生第十九》

P186 祝宗人玄端以临牢筴，说彘曰："汝奚恶死？吾将三月豢汝，十日戒，三日斋，藉白茅，加汝肩尻乎彫俎之上，则汝为之乎？"为彘谋，曰不如食以糠糟而错之牢筴之中，自为谋，则苟生有轩冕之尊，死得于腠楯之上、聚偻之中则为之。为彘谋则去之，自为谋则取之，所异彘者何也？

《庄子◎达生第十九》

P187 孔子观于吕梁，县水三十仞，流沫四十里，鼋鼍鱼鳖之所不能游也。见一丈夫游之，以为有苦而欲死也，使弟子并流而拯之。数百步而出，被发行歌而游于塘下。

孔子从而问焉，曰："吾以子为鬼，察子则人也。请问，蹈水有道乎？"曰："亡，吾无道。吾始乎故，长乎性，成乎命。与齐俱入，与汩皆出，从水之道而不为私焉。此吾所以蹈之也。"

《庄子◎达生第十九》

P188 梓庆削木为鐻，鐻成，见者惊犹鬼神。鲁侯见而问焉，曰："子何术以为焉？"

对曰："臣工人，何术之有！虽然，有一焉。臣将为鐻，未尝敢以耗气也，必斋以静心。斋三日，而不敢怀庆赏爵禄；斋五日，不敢怀非誉巧拙；斋七日，辄然忘吾有四枝形体也。当是时也，无公朝，其巧专而外滑消；然后入山林，观天性；形躯至矣，然后成见鐻，然后加手焉；不然则已。则以天合天，器之所以疑神者，其由是与！"

《庄子◎达生第十九》

P189 东野稷以御见庄公，进退中绳，左右旋中规。庄公以为文弗过也，使人钩百而反。

颜阖遇之，入见曰："稷之马将败。"公密而不应。

少焉，果败而反。公曰："子何以知之？"

曰："其马力竭矣。而犹求焉，故曰败。"

245

《庄子◎达生第十九》

P190 工倕旋而盖规矩，指与物化，而不以心稽，故其灵台，一而不桎。忘足，履之适也；忘要，带之适也；忘是非，心之适也；不内变，不外从，事会之适也。始乎适而未尝不适者，忘适之适也。

《庄子◎达生第十九》

P191 庄子衣大布而补之，正廑系履而过魏王。魏王曰："何先生之惫邪？"庄子曰："贫也，非惫也。士有道德不能行，惫也；衣弊履穿，贫也，非惫也；此所谓非遭时也。王独不见夫腾猿乎？其得枏梓豫章也，揽蔓其枝而王长其间，虽羿，蓬蒙不能眄睨也。及其得柘棘枳枸之间也，危行侧视，振动悼栗；此筋骨非有加急而不柔也，处势不便，未足以逞其能也。今处昏上乱相之间，而欲无惫，奚可得邪？此比干之见剖心，徵也夫！"

《庄子◎山木第二十》

P192-P193 庄子见鲁哀公。哀公曰："鲁多儒士，少为先生方者。"
庄子曰："鲁少儒。"
哀公曰："举鲁国而儒服，何谓少乎？"
庄子曰："周闻之，儒者冠圜冠者，知天时；履句屦者，知地形；缓佩玦者，事至而断。君子有其道者，未必为其服也；为其服者；未必知其道也。公固以为不然，何不号于国中曰："无此道而为此服者，其罪死？""
于是哀公号之五日，而鲁国无敢儒服者，独有一丈夫儒服而立乎公门。公即召而问以国事，千转万变而不穷。
庄子曰："以鲁国而儒者一人耳，可谓多乎？"

《庄子◎田子方第二十一》

P194 百里奚爵禄不入于心，故饭牛而牛肥，使秦穆公忘其贱，与之政也。有虞氏死生不入于心，故足以动人。

《庄子◎田子方第二十一》

P195 宋元君将画图，众史皆至，受揖而立；舐笔和墨，在外者半。有一史后至者，儃儃然不趋，受揖不立，因之舍。公使人视之，则解衣槃礴臝。君曰：可矣，是真画者也。"

《庄子◎田子方第二十一》

P196-P197 列御寇为伯昏无人射，引之盈贯，措杯水其肘上，发之，适矢复沓，方矢复寓。当是时，犹象人也。
伯昏无人曰："是射之射，非不射之射也。尝与汝登高山，履危石，临百仞之渊，若能射乎？"
于是无人遂登高山，履危石，临百仞之渊，背逡巡，足二分垂在外，揖御寇而进之。御寇伏地，汗流至踵。
伯昏无人曰："夫至人者，上窥青天，下潜黄泉，挥斥八极，神气不变。今汝怵然有恂目之志，尔于中也殆矣夫！"

《庄子◎田子方第二十一》

P198 肩吾问于孙叔敖说："子三为令尹而不荣华，三去之而无忧色。吾始也疑子，今视子之鼻间栩栩然，子之用心独奈何？"

孙叔敖曰："吾何以过人哉！吾以其来不可却也，其去不可止也，吾以为得失之非我也，而无忧色而已矣。我何以过人哉！且不知其在彼乎，其在我乎？其在彼邪？亡乎我；在我邪？亡乎彼。方将踌躇，方将四顾，何暇至乎人贵人贱哉！"

《庄子◎田子方第二十一》

P199 舜问乎丞曰："道可得而有乎？"

曰："汝身非汝有也，汝何得有夫道？"

舜曰："吾身非吾有也，孰有之哉？"

曰："是天地之委形也；生非汝有，是天地之委和也；性命非汝有，是天地之委顺也；子孙非汝有，是天地之委蜕也。故行不知所在，处不知所持，食不知所味。天地之强阳气也，又胡可得而有邪！

《庄子◎知北游第二十二》

P200-P201 东郭子问于庄子曰："所谓道，恶乎在？"庄子曰："无所不在。"

东郭子曰："期而后可。"庄子曰："在蝼蚁。"曰："何其下邪？"曰："在稊稗。"曰："何其愈下邪？"曰："在瓦甓。"曰："何其愈甚邪？"曰："在屎溺。"东郭子不应。

庄子曰："夫子之问也，固不及质。正获之问于监市履狶也，每下愈况。汝唯莫必，无乎逃物。至道若是，大言亦然。周遍咸三者，异名同实，其指一也。"

尝相与游乎无何有之宫，同合而论，无所终穷乎，尝相与无为乎！澹而静乎！漠而清乎！调而闲乎！寥已吾志，无往焉而不知其所至，去而来而不知其所止，吾已往来焉而不知其所终；彷徨乎冯闳，大知入焉而不知其所穷。物物者与物无际，而物有际者，所谓物际者也；不际之际，际之不际者也。谓盈虚衰杀，彼为盈虚非盈虚，彼为衰杀非衰杀，彼为本末非本末，彼为积散非积散也。

《庄子◎知北游第二十二》

P202-P203 泰清问乎无穷曰："子知道乎？"无穷曰："吾不知。"又问乎无为。无为曰："吾知道。"曰："子之知道，亦有数乎？"曰："有。"曰："其数若何？"

无为曰："吾知道之可以贵，可以贱，可以约，可以散，此吾所以知道之数也。"泰清以之言也问乎无始曰："若是，则无穷之弗知与无为之知，孰是而孰非也？"无始曰："不知深矣，知之浅矣；弗知内矣，知之外矣。"

于是泰清中而叹曰："弗知乃知乎！知乃不知乎！孰知不知之知？"

无始曰："道不可闻，闻而非也；道不可见，见而非也；道不可言，言而非也。知形形之不形乎！道不当名。"

无始曰："有问道而应之者，不知道也。虽问道者，亦未闻道。道无问，问无应。无问问之，是问穷也；无应应之，是无内也。以无内待问穷。若是者，外不观乎宇宙，内不知乎大初，是以不过乎昆仑，不游乎太虚。"

《庄子◎知北游第二十二》

P204 大马之捶钩者，年八十矣，而不失豪芒。大马曰："子巧与？有道与？"

曰："臣有守也。臣之年二十而好捶钩，于物无视也，非钩无察也。是用之者，假不用者也以长得其用，而况乎无不用者乎！物孰不资焉！"

《庄子◎知北游第二十二》

P205 学者，学其所不能学也；行者，行其所不能行也；辩者，辩其所不能辩也。知止乎其所不能知，至矣；若有不即是者，天钧败之。

《庄子◎庚桑楚第二十三》

P206 蹍市人之足，则辞以放骜，兄则以妪，大亲则已矣。故曰：至礼有不人，至义不物，至知不谋，至仁无亲，至信辟金。

《庄子◎庚桑楚第二十三》

P207-P208 徐无鬼因女商见魏武侯，武侯劳之曰："先生病矣！苦于山林之劳，故乃肯见于寡人。"

徐无鬼曰："我则劳于君，君有何劳于我！君将盈耆欲，长好恶，则性命之情病矣；君将黜耆欲，掔好恶，则耳目病矣。我将劳君，君有何劳于我！"武侯超然不对。

少焉，徐无鬼曰："尝语君，吾相狗也。下之质执饱而止，是狸德；中之质若视日，上之质，若亡其一。吾相狗，又不若吾相马也。吾相马，直者中绳，曲者中钩，方者中矩，圆者中规，是国马也，而未若天下马也。天下马有成材，若恤若失，若丧其一，若是者，超轶绝尘，不知其所。"武侯大悦而笑。

《庄子◎徐无鬼第二十四》

P209-P210 徐无鬼出，女商曰："先生独何以说吾君乎？吾所以说吾君者，横说之则以诗书礼乐，从说之则以金板六弢，奉事而大有功者不可为数，而吾君未尝启齿。今先生何以说吾君，使吾君说若此乎？"

徐无鬼曰："吾直告之吾相狗马耳。"

女商曰："若是乎？"

曰："子不闻夫越之流人乎？去国数日，见其所知而喜；去国旬月，见所尝见于国中者喜；及期年也，见似人者而喜矣；不亦去人滋久，思人滋深乎？夫逃虚空者，藜藋柱乎鼪鼬之迳，踉位其空，闻人足音跫然而喜矣，又况乎昆弟亲戚之謦欬其侧者乎！久矣夫，莫以真人之言謦欬吾之侧乎！"

《庄子◎徐无鬼第二十四》

P211 吴王浮于江，登乎狙之山。众狙见之，恂然弃而走，逃于深蓁，有一狙焉，委蛇攫搔，见巧乎王。王射之，敏给搏捷矢。王命相者趋射之，狙执死。

王顾谓其友颜不疑曰："之狙也，伐其巧，恃其便以敖予，以至此殛也！戒之哉！嗟乎，无以汝色骄人哉！"颜不疑归而师董梧以锄其色，去乐辞显，三年而国人称之。

《庄子◎徐无鬼第二十四》

P212 故足之于地也践，虽践，恃其所不蹍而后善博也；人之于知也少，虽少，恃其所不知而后知天之所谓也。知大一，知大阴，知大目，知大均，知大方，知大信，知大定，至矣。大一通之，大阴解之，大目视之，大均缘之，大方体之，大信稽之，大定持之。

尽有天，循有照，冥有枢，始有彼。则其解之也似不解之者，其知之也似不知之也，不知而后知之。

《庄子◎徐无鬼第二十四》

P213 冉相氏得其环中以随成，与物无终无始，无几无时。日与物化者，一不化者也，阖尝舍之！夫师天而不得师天，与物皆殉，其以为事也若之何？夫圣人未始有天，未始有人，未始有始，未始有物，与世偕行而不替，所行之备而不洫，其合之也若之何？

《庄子◎则阳第二十五》

P214 任公子为大钩巨缁，五十犗以为饵，蹲乎会稽，投竿东海，旦旦而钓，期年不得鱼。已而大鱼食之，牵巨钩，锚没而下，骛扬而奋鬐，白波若山，海水震荡，声侔鬼神，惮赫千里。任公子得若鱼，离而腊之，自制河以东，苍梧已北，莫不厌若鱼者。已而后世辁才讽说之徒，皆惊而相告也。夫揭竿累，趋灌渎，守鲵鲋，其于得大鱼难矣。饰小说以干县令，其于大达亦远矣。是以未尝闻任氏之风俗，其不可与经于世亦远矣。

《庄子◎外物第二十六》

P215-P216 庄子谓惠子曰："孔子行年六十而六十化，始时所是，卒而非之，未知今之所谓是之非五十九非也。"

惠子曰："孔子勤志服知也。"

庄子曰："孔子谢之矣，而其未之尝言。孔子云：'夫受才乎大本，复灵以生。鸣而当律，言而当法，利义陈乎前，而好恶是非直服人之口而已矣。使人乃以心服，而不敢蘁立，定天下之定。'已乎已乎！吾且不得及彼乎！"

曾子再仕而心再化，曰："吾及亲仕，三釜而心乐；后仕，三千钟而不洎亲，吾心悲。"

弟子问于仲尼曰："若参者，可谓无所县其罪乎？"

曰："既已县矣。夫无所县者，可以有哀乎？彼视三釜三千钟，如观鸟雀蚊虻相过乎前也。"

《庄子◎寓言第二十七》

P217 颜成子游谓东郭子綦曰："自吾闻子之言，一年而野，二年而从，三年而通，四年而物，五年而来，六年而鬼入，七年而天成，八年而不知死，不知生，九年而大妙。"

《庄子◎寓言第二十七》

P218 尧以天下让许由，许由不受。又让于子州支父，子州支父曰："以我为天子，犹之可也。虽然，我适有幽忧之病，方且治之，未暇治天下也。"夫天下至重也，而不以害其生，又况他物乎！唯无以天下为者，可以托天下也。

《庄子◎让王第二十八》

P219 楚昭王失国，屠羊说走而从于昭王。昭王反国，将赏从者，及屠羊说。屠羊说曰："大王失国，说失屠羊；大王反国，说亦反屠羊。臣之爵禄已复矣，又何赏之有哉！"

王曰："强之！"

屠羊说曰："大国失国，非臣之罪，故不敢伏其诛；大王反国，非臣之功，故不敢当其赏。"

《庄子◎让王第二十八》

P220 孔子谓颜回曰："回，来！家贫居卑，胡不仕乎？"

颜回对曰："不愿仕。回有郭外之田五十亩，足以给飦粥；郭内之田十亩，足以为丝麻；鼓琴足以自娱，所学夫子之道者足以自乐也。回不愿仕。"

孔子愀然变容曰："善哉回之意！丘闻之，'知足者不以利自累也，审自得者失之而不惧，行修于内者无位而不怍。'丘诵之久矣，今于回而后见之，是丘之得也。"

《庄子◎让王第二十八》

P221 宋人有曹商者，为宋王使秦。其往也，得车数乘；王说之，益车百乘。反于宋，见庄子曰："夫处穷闾阨巷，困窘织屦，槁项黄馘者，商之所短也；一悟万乘之主而从车百乘者，商之所长也。"

庄子曰："秦王有病召医，破痈溃痤者得车一乘，舐痔者得车五乘，所治愈下，得车愈多。子岂治其痔邪，何得车之多也？子行矣！"

《庄子◎列御寇第三十二》